WOLF CREEK CIDER

The Story of Aaron Stroud

MARK GENGLER

WOLF CREEK CIDER, *The Story of Aaron Stroud*
by Mark Gengler

Published by

 SOUL FIRE PRESS
PO Box 571
Gleneden Beach, OR 97388

Interior layout, cover design by Suzanne Parrott
Cover art, *"Autumn wine barrels..."*, ©OlgaChernyak, Shutterstock.com / royalty-free stock image ID: 701560051

Genre: *Young Adult, stock market crash, depression, apple cider, Logan Street Bridge disaster, Merrill, Wisconsin*

ISBN: 978-1-944072-05-6 (pb)

10 9 8 7 6 5 4 3 2 1

Printed in the
United States of America

WOLF CREEK CIDER

The Story of Aaron Stroud

MARK GENGLER

SOUL FIRE PRESS

ACKNOWLEDGMENTS

No author has ever written a novel alone. I owe many thank yous to many people. To Suzanne, my new publisher and editor who took the time to get to know me and give me much needed advice and help. My wife Mary the 'computer widow' when I really get into the meat of the story. To Kim, Maria, Jacob and Shelly who got me through some tough mornings with smiles and hot coffee. To my brother and sisters, nieces and nephews, cousins and their extended families who give me encouragement and ideas for the next novel. To my friends Reggie and Judy for just being there when I need a shoulder to lean on. All of you helped make this possible.

*This novel is dedicated to my grand-parents,
my parents and all my Uncles and Aunts who lived through
and survived one of the worst periods of American history.*

*As a child, I remember them talking about a dollar a day
wages, pulling together to get by and praying things
would get better.*

*Their generation saw the banks close and neighbors
lose their farms. The Civilian Conservation Corps
helped my Father and Uncles to feed and cloth their families.*

*I thank each one of them for the values
they passed on to their children.*

CHAPTER ONE

"Damn this thing!" I was never happy about dressing up in a suit because I never learned how to knot a tie properly. Today was different. Today I was getting married. Looking in the mirror, I saw a nervous 22-year-old brown-haired man with beads of sweat forming by his hairline. The suit fit my six-foot frame although a little tight across the shoulders, but all my clothes fit like that. I heard the Model T Ford pull up outside and knew Dad was here. Reuben Stroud was a stocky six footer with iron grey hair and gnarled hands—the end product of years spent building bridges across Michigan. Right now we were in Lansing and Dad was working on the new steel bridge across the Grand River, known as the South Logan Street bridge.

The outside door opened, and Dad walked in. With a slight smile, he gently took my tie in his hands, and in ten seconds, it was perfectly knotted. "Let's get a move on son. Your bride is waiting."

Six months ago, I had proposed to the prettiest girl in Lansing named Ardyce Johnson. Today, April 1, 1929, she would become Mrs. Aaron Stroud.

We piled into the Ford and headed for the church. "This is one of the days when I wish your mother were still here,"

Dad sighed. I wished it too. We lost Mom during the Flu epidemic in 1919. I was only twelve, and it hit me almost as hard as it did Dad. He had never remarried, keeping her picture on his bedroom dresser.

I don't remember much about the wedding ceremony. My whole being focused on the lovely face framed by soft, dark hair, topped by the white tiara with a lace veil. At five-foot-six, her head fit nicely under my chin. She was perfect.

After our vows, the church organ burst into full volume as we strolled down the aisle with her parents and my dad following behind. Hugs and kisses for the bride and hand-shakes and back-slapping for the groom went on for a half an hour on the church steps.

From somewhere in the crowd, a voice hollered, "Let's get to the reception at the Union Hall; don't want all that food to spoil!"

With a little laugh, Ardyce squeezed my hand and whis-pered, "We better get going; my Uncle Joe is hungry."

Dad led the parade, followed by my new in-laws, Bernard and Eunice Johnson. With much shouting and horn honk-ing, we drove slowly down Water Street to the Hall.

After Mom passed, Dad rented a small two-bedroom house with a kitchen, bath, and family room—comfortable for two men. A bridge builder's life is nomadic—moving from job to job. For this reason, Dad had never bought a house that could be called a family home. Most new bridg-es took at least two years to construct, sometimes more de-pending on the span. Replacing old wooden trestle bridges with modern steel bridges meant removing the old structures down to bedrock and starting all over.

The process started with digging coffer dams to hold back the water while concrete was poured to hold the new steel pilings in place.

From the age of sixteen, I drove one of the trucks hauling supplies from the train station to the work-site. The steel came from Bethlehem, Pennsylvania and was contracted for by the American Bridge Company. Dad had begun working for the Keystone Bridge Company as a 19-year-old young man. When Carnegie sold out his steel mills to Morgan, the name changed, but business went on as usual.

CHAPTER TWO

Early one morning, as I waited for the crane to load my truck, the distinctive booming and shrieking sound of steel giving way pierced my soul. I jumped into the vehicle and sped toward the bridgehead.

I watched in horror as the entire structure shook like a wet dog and then slowly toppled into the rushing water. Men, driven by adrenaline and instinct, rushed in, barking orders: "Get some ropes!"

"Pull that man out of the river!"

Disaster quickly evolved into a rescue effort. Hours later, a handful of lifeless bodies lay on the shore—one of which was my father, Reuben Stroud.

Altogether, we lost six men and two severely injured on that fatal day, April 12, 1929. Bridge inspectors would later report that one of the cofferdams had given way, allowing the river to wash away the fresh concrete, causing the half-complete structure to collapse.

It was a perfectly beautiful day for such a somber event. Two of the bodies left on the afternoon train, heading back to their hometowns for burial. The other four, including Dad, were being laid to rest at St. John's cemetery here in

Lansing. It felt odd wearing the same suit to the funeral that I had worn just twelve days before to our wedding. As they lowered caskets into the graves, the church bell tolled their last goodbye.

Later that afternoon, as Ardyce and I enjoyed coffee on the front porch, a new black Packard came to a slow stop in front of the house. The driver got out, went around the vehicle, and opened the rear passenger door.

A portly man wearing a dark blue suit with a matching Homburg hat and carrying a black briefcase stepped from the vehicle.

"Are you Aaron Stroud, son of Reuben Stroud?" he asked as he stepped onto the porch.

"I'm Aaron, and this is my wife, Ardyce," I replied.

Removing his hat, he shook my hand and stated, "I am Edwin Soames from the American Bridge Company. I wish to offer my condolences on the tragic death of your father."

"Please, come into the house. May I take your hat and offer you a cup of coffee?" asked Ardyce.

With a slight bow, Mr. Soames handed her his hat. "A cup of coffee would go well, then we have some business to take care of," he answered.

Seated around the kitchen table, Mr. Soames explained his visit. "We at the American Bridge Company understand your occupation is often a dangerous one. We urge all our employees to take out an insurance policy in the event of an accident. Your father has had a policy for years." Opening his briefcase, he took out some papers. "Reuben had a $1500 policy in case of an accident. In the case of death, that payment is doubled."

I was stunned! Dad had never mentioned any insurance. My hand shook as I accepted the check for $3000 from Mr. Soames. I looked at Ardyce. Her hand covered her mouth, her eyes wide with disbelief.

"I will need you to sign some papers to acknowledge payment," Mr. Soames continued, "also any funeral debts incurred will be paid by our Company." With a shaking hand, I signed the papers. Sliding them back into the briefcase, Mr. Soames said, "I must leave, as I have two other families to attend to." We walked him to the door and watched as he drove away.

CHAPTER THREE

Families dread sorting through the belongings of the deceased. It is a struggle to choose what parts of a person's life to donate, keep, or throw away. Everything is precious—a part of a lost loved one. Yet, they are only materials possessions.

I started with the closet and Dad's firearms. Three gun cases held the marlin lever action .22, a Winchester Model 97 pump shotgun and a Springfield bolt action .30-06. These would now become mine.

Leaving the clothing for last, I lay the weapons on the bed and turned to the dresser drawers, starting at the bottom and working my way up. The first drawers held nothing out of the ordinary. When I reached the top drawer, my heart skipped a beat as I found keepsakes from my mother: her wedding ring, a necklace with a pair of matching earrings and a small brooch. Nestled among them were a little loose change, an old Ingersoll pocket watch, the pipe I had given Dad at Christmas, and a packet of papers tied with a blue ribbon. I blinked away tears when Ardyce entered the room, laid her small hand on my shoulder, and kissed my forehead. Without her by my side, I am not sure I could have survived this ordeal.

"I'm sure Dad would want you to have these," I said as I handed her Mom's jewelry.

"Aaron, these are lovely," she gasped as she held them in her hands.

I untied the ribbon holding the papers together: Dad and Mom's marriage license, my birth certificate, a copy of the insurance policy, the title to the Model T, my High School Diploma, and two envelopes. The first envelope contained three one hundred bills, a fifty and a twenty—Dad's savings.

"Because we moved from job to job, Dad never used a bank. He did all his business in cash," I said.

With a slight nod of her head, she replied, "My Uncle Joe is the same way. He keeps his savings in an old coffee can under the kitchen sink."

The second envelope was sealed and fairly thick. Using my pocket knife, I slit open the envelope and dumped the contents out on the bed. The first thing that caught my eye was a folded paper with the word 'DEED' in bold print.

Unfolding it, I read slowly as Ardyce sorted through the other papers. In amazement, I almost whispered, "This is a deed to a 40-acre parcel of land in Wisconsin!"

Holding up the rest of the papers, Ardyce breathlessly replied, "These are the tax records and a plat map. Did you know about this?"

I sat down at the kitchen table as my lovely wife brewed a pot of coffee. "I knew Dad was born in Wisconsin, and he met my Mom there while working on the bridge across the Wisconsin River at Merrill."

"Do you have family there," she asked.

"The only family Dad ever mentioned was a younger brother who was killed in the great war," I said.

With a little frown, she asked, "Why would he buy land in Lincoln County, Wisconsin?"

"I remember a few times, while I was growing up, Dad somehow managed to get a week or ten days off. We'd take the train to Chicago, then north to Wausau. From there we rented a horse and buggy and went fishing or hunting, depending on the time of year." I crooked a smile, remembering how Dad had loved those trips. "I'll bet the old man planned to retire there in a few years. The deed says there is a house and barn. It sure would be nice to see the property at least."

With growing excitement in her voice, Ardyce said, "Let's do it! We could take a two-week honeymoon, drive to Wisconsin, and see if the land is worth keeping."

Mulling it over, the idea appealed to me! Why not take some time to explore my dad's dream? Looking out the kitchen window, I could see Dad's Model T sitting on four almost-bald tires. Following my gaze, Ardyce said, "That Ford will never make the trip. Let's go see my father and trade it in on something newer, something that will get us there and back!" My father-in-law, Bernard Johnson, ran the only Ford dealership in town. With the right auto, we could be on our way to a real adventure!

CHAPTER FOUR

Bernard Johnson stood a stout 5-foot 10-inches. A slightly balding man who always seemed to have a smile on his tanned face. Ardyce told him about the property in Wisconsin and our plans to visit it. "I think it's a wonderful idea," he said. "You two need some fun time together, and this trip could open a whole new world for you. Do you plan to take the train?"

"No, father, that's why we came to see you," said Ardyce. "Reuben's Model T isn't the car for this trip. We were hoping you could find us a vehicle up to the task."

Bernard stroked his chin for a moment, and then his eyes lit up! "You two have no idea how lucky you are! I have exactly what you need. Come with me!" Following him outside and around to the back of the garage, we saw three autos awaiting us: A Packard Touring car, a flatbed Chevrolet truck, and a Ford Panel van. Giving each other a puzzled look, Ardyce and I wondered just what her father had in mind.

"That panel van is going to be your home away from home on your journey," Bernard explained. "I can only imagine what the roads are like between here and the middle of Wisconsin. This van has a heavy-duty suspension, an eight-cylinder engine and the cab is enclosed."

Stepping forward, I opened the back doors and looked inside. Ardyce, on her hands and knees, climbed in and sat down. "It certainly is roomy, but why this one and not the truck?"

With a big smile, Bernard said, "It came to me almost like a vision! Your uncle Joe is the best carpenter in Lansing. As a wedding present, I'm going to have him turn this into a traveling home. A folding bed, slim cupboards with doors, storage space for cooking equipment, a locker for food and two five-gallon jerry cans, one for water and one for gasoline!"

As he laid out his plan, I could see it take shape before me. Looking at the side of the van, Ardyce pointed and said, "If uncle Joe can put a small window with a screen here, we will have fresh air all night."

Bernard had pulled a small notebook from his pants pocket and was scribbling furiously. Scratching his head a bit, he crossed something out and wrote a final time. "What year is Reuben's Model T?" he asked.

I thought a minute and replied, "It's a 1925 and still in pretty good shape."

Very seriously, Bernard informed us, "I can let you have this panel van for $300 plus the Model T. Joe and I will split the cost of fixing it up, and that might take two weeks. Does that fit your budget?"

"Dad left us some savings that will pay for it," I said, looking at Ardyce. She was all smiles, and I could almost see the plans running through her head.

Hugging her father, she said, "Thanks for this, and tell mother we will be over for supper Friday night." I handed Bernard the three one hundred dollar bills from Dad's savings.

We drove to the bank and opened a savings account. American Bridge Company deposited the check, and the bank gave us a small brown book to show the balance.

"I think we should do some shopping for things we will need," said Ardyce.

"Good idea," I agreed. "But first, I need to stop by the bridge site and let them know I will be gone for a while."

The boss on the job, Nelson Gant, told me to take as much time as I needed, shook my hand, handed me my last paycheck and wished me well.

The hardware store was our next stop. We found an outdoor iron grate with folding legs to set over a fire to cook. Ardyce picked out a complete set of metal cookware that came with a coffee pot, skillet, plates, cups, utensils, and salt & pepper shakers. We also found an ax, a hatchet, a shovel, and fifty feet of rope. With a finger on her chin, Ardyce mused, "What if we get stuck in some mud?"

I went back and got a 25-foot tow chain. Toting our haul to the counter took two trips. Mr. Gilman started adding it up and commented, "Going on a camping trip it looks like."

"More like a camping adventure," I replied. The bill was $19.23. We loaded everything into the Model T and headed home.

CHAPTER FIVE

The next two weeks dragged by as we decided what to take. The food list was the main topic of discussion: a small cured ham, a slab of bacon, canned corn, hash, beans, fruit, and tomatoes. A bag of potatoes, some onions, baking powder, a bag of flour and a small box of cheese seemed to be all we would need. I searched the closet shelf and found Dad's old Buck hunting knife in its leather sheath. The guns in their cases would also go along. We each packed three changes of clothing in our shared suitcase. A good pair of Redwing boots for each and the list seemed complete. Ardyce was an excellent cook but took along a cookbook titled 'Outdoor cooking,' just to be sure. On a Friday in the third week of June, we drove to her father's dealership to check on the van.

When we arrived, Bernard was deep into a sales talk with Pastor Pettigrew from the Lutheran church. He waved us in and then pointed to the back of the garage area. "I'll be with you in a minute," he spoke quietly as we passed by.

Opening the back door we saw the Packard was still there, the flatbed truck was gone and there sat our Ford van. Before opening the back doors, we walked around the van and noticed some changes.

"Look, Aaron. Uncle Joe put a small window on each side," Ardyce said with surprise. They were about 18-inch square with an outside screen. It made sense. With the hot months to come, the cross-ventilation would be welcome. On the driver side, a red five-gallon can was mounted by the front fender to carry spare gasoline. On the passenger side, sat a similar can, painted blue, would hold our water supply. On the front, over the radiator, the spare tire on its rim sat securely between the headlights. In the rear, a trailer hitch stuck out that had not been there before. Opening the rear doors, we both gasped in surprise.

"How do you like it?" Bernard said as he strode up with a big smile.

The layout was remarkable. Along both sides of the vehicle were slim cabinets with wire mesh in framed doors. They stuck out about eight or nine inches, leaving room to move around. Beneath the cabinets were wooden chests, three on each side. The really eye-catching thing was the bed. A mattress lay on a wooden frame. Looking closer, I saw hinges on each side.

"The bed folds up," I said to Ardyce. Laughing with glee, Bernard showed us how to fold the bed and latch it down with hook and eye attachments. Stout wooden legs, a foot long, kept it off the floor.

"This will give you both plenty of room to move around before bedtime," Bernard pointed out, "and the chests will hold your clothing, bedding, food and any other gear you have."

Ardyce threw her arms around her father. With tears in her eyes, she cried, "It's perfect, just perfect! Thank you so much!"

I shook Bernard's hand. "We will spend the night packing up and leave at first light tomorrow," I told him.

CHAPTER SIX

As the first pale light of dawn pushed the darkness away, we drove southwest out of Lansing. A short stop for pancakes and coffee at a roadside diner, then back on the road. Our goal was to make the town of Buchanan at the Indiana border by dusk.

The roads were in good shape, mostly graveled and graded. The sun rose into a cloudless sky as we motored past Kalamazoo. About a half-hour past Portage, we saw a sign for a campground.

"Let's stop for lunch here," Ardyce said, pointing at the sign. We pulled over and parked by the small shack used as an office. An older man ambled out puffing on a pipe.

"You folks looking for a campsite?" he asked.

Getting out to stretch, I answered, "No, sir. We thought we would just have some lunch and keep going."

"Well, help yourselves to the water and the outhouse," he replied and went back inside.

Ardyce spread a towel on a picnic table and laid out a loaf of homemade bread, sweet butter, the cured ham, and the cheese box. I filled our small water jug at the hand pump and fetched two cups from the van. Two ham and cheese sandwiches apiece took the edge off of our hunger. Packing everything back up we stopped by the outhouse, and then we were back on the road.

Roadside vegetable stands, farmers working knee-high cornfields, small herds of cows, all of Michigan going about its daily business as we drove by. Ardyce was humming something familiar.

"Sing that for me," I said. Ardyce had a lovely voice that soothed me each time I heard it. She sang 'Over there,' one of the popular songs from the great war.

As the afternoon wore on, we slowly drove through Schoolcraft, a sleepy town with only one stop sign on Main street. As the sun began its slow descent, the heat of the day eased a bit. I drove to a Standard station for gas in Buchanan. We stopped for the night at a campground just before the Indiana border. I paid the lady in the office two dollars for a site with a picnic table and a fire pit. Ardyce filled the coffeepot at the pump while I got an armload of wood from the woodpile. When the wood was half-burned down to glowing embers, I set up the iron grate. Out came the frying pans as the coffee heated up.

Gray shadows drifted across the dying campfire as we cleaned up the pans and plates. Packing everything away except the blue-enamel dishpan, I heated more water for Ardyce. She washed the road dust off in the van, and then it was my turn. By the time I finished, Ardyce had the bed made and turned down. Somehow we both managed to sleep comfortably on the single bed mattress. The light breeze through the windows was welcome.

The sun peeked through the treetops when I awoke, alone. I dressed quickly and stepped out of the van. Ardyce was busy, elbow-deep in flour at the picnic table.

"I'm making biscuits, and the coffee is ready," she informed me. Beside her on the table was the outdoor cookbook which she glanced at from time to time. As she formed the dough, she laid each one in the Dutch oven until it was full. Placing the cover on, she set the oven on the grate to bake. In no time, we had perfect biscuits with butter and some of her mother's homemade strawberry jam.

"You are becoming quite the outdoor cook," I said, buttering my third biscuit.

With a shy smile, she answered, "This is the most wonderful time of my life, and I intend to enjoy every minute of it."

CHAPTER SEVEN

We crossed the border into Indiana, where the road needed repair. Ruts, potholes, and places we had to detour around to avoid the muddy stretches. As we entered Illinois, the road improved enough for us to make up some time.

Driving around Chicago, we stopped for lunch at a diner on the north side of Elgin. Over hamburgers and Coca-Colas, we studied the Wisconsin map. "If the roads are good, we should make Lake Geneva by sundown," Ardyce said between bites.

"We will need to stop for gas around Kenosha," I said. A restroom visit and back on the road.

As the miles rolled by, another cloudless day blessed us. Fields of corn, some winter wheat ready for the harvest, the occasional horse and buggy traffic as well as a few trucks.

"Sing for me, honey," I said.

Her beautiful voice soon settled on 'Sweet Georgia Brown,' then one of my favorites, 'Barney Google.'

A little after four o'clock, we saw the waters of Lake Geneva off to our right—a popular vacation town for many and home to some very well-to-do families. Smiling at my lovely bride, I asked, "Would you like it if we stayed the night at a motor-court and maybe took a hot shower and slept in a bigger bed?"

Laughing and clapping her hands, she replied, "I was going to suggest that very thing. Let's find one with a diner and have supper."

The Sunset Motor Court on the north end of the lake was our stop for the night. For ten dollars, we got a cozy cabin with a bathroom. I carried in our suitcase as Ardyce opened some windows. She claimed the shower first, found her soap and shampoo and a half-hour later emerged wrapped in a large towel.

"I love our van, but this is what I needed," she sighed.

Picking up my razor, brush, and shaving mug, I took my turn, hoping there was a dry towel for me. There was!

Dressed in clean clothes, we spread open the map of Wisconsin and traced our route.

"How long before we reach Merrill?" Ardyce asked. Merrill was the closest town to the property on Wolf creek.

"Two more days on the road should do it," I answered. I knew we would have to stop at the Courthouse in Merrill to transfer the deed from Dad's name to mine. Many thoughts crowded my thinking. What condition were the buildings? Could the land be tilled and farmed? Were there any close neighbors? Was any of the property wooded?

Ruffling my hair, Ardyce scolded, "Stop thinking and start relaxing. Let's go check out that Diner, I'm hungry!"

We left the motor-court at 6 a.m., drove into Elkhorn for gas and had breakfast at a Café on the north end of town. The roads were in good shape, and we made good time. We passed a farmer and his son mending fence, two boys with cane poles over their shoulders, a milk truck loaded with cans and a team of horses pulling a wagon. There were a few other autos, mostly headed south.

Checking the map, Ardyce motioned me to turn left. "We need to get onto highway 51, which will take us right into Merrill."

We got onto highway 51 by Lake Monona and turned the panel van north. The day passed quickly as the Ford ate up the miles. Gassing up at a crossroads, we bought candy bars and soft drinks for lunch. By six in the evening, we could see Stevens Point just ahead. Another mile took us to a campground.

Parking the Ford, we got out took a long-deserved stretch. Ardyce paid for the campsite while I gathered wood for the fire. Fried ham and potatoes with coffee made a fine supper.

The first stars came out as we finished our coffee at the picnic table. "I almost wish this trip didn't have to end," Ardyce said softly.

Putting my arm around her shoulder, I pulled her closer. "Let's see what tomorrow brings," I whispered in her ear. We moved into the van, made up the bed, and settled in for the night.

Before the sun was up, we were on the road. A diner in Knowlton was open, so we stopped for breakfast. Over pancakes and bacon, we traced our route.

"Wausau is the next big town, then into Merrill," I said as my finger moved up the map.

"What time do you think we will get there?" Ardyce asked.

"With a little luck and good roads, we should arrive early afternoon." As I paid the cashier, I inquired, "How good is the road to Merrill?"

Giving a little snort, she replied, "The road ain't too bad, just don't get run over by one of those damn loggin' trucks."

We found out later what she meant. Wausau was a town built on sawmills. Every other vehicle on the rutted road was some kind of truck hauling logs. By noon, we cleared the north end of town, and the traffic in our lane dropped off considerably.

We reached Merrill just before three o'clock and parked in front of the Lincoln County courthouse. The land and deeds office was open with an older gentleman operating the counter. After showing him Dad's death certificate, he transferred the ownership to me, handed me the new deed, a plat map, a set of keys, and charged me three dollars.

CHAPTER EIGHT

Walking out of the courthouse arm in arm, I asked Ardyce, "Does a motor-court sound good for tonight?"

With a laugh, she replied, "If the new Land Baron wishes to treat his wife to some luxury, she does not object!"

Baxter's Motor Court charged ten dollars a night and offered the use of their washing machine. As I unpacked, she showered and dressed. While I was showering, she gathered up the laundry and left, returning a half-hour later with a borrowed basket holding the damp clothes and a small bag of clothespins.

I helped to hang the clothes to dry on the line. "Lucy, at the office, said the restaurant in Merrill has a roast beef special today that is really good." Looking at my pocket watch, I realized it was almost six o'clock. A roast beef supper would hit the spot.

The clothes were dry by the time we got back to our cabin. We took them all in, and Ardyce folded them while I returned the basket.

"What time are you folks leaving in the morning," asked Mrs. Lucy Baxter.

"Probably about 5:30," I told her.

"I'll be up making coffee and fresh cinnamon rolls, if you care to stop by," she offered.

"Thank you, we would love to," I said with a big smile.

Walking from the cabin to the office the next morning, the delicious aroma of hot cinnamon rolls drifted out of the open kitchen window.

"Come in and have a chair," Lucy called, "I'm icing the rolls, so pour us some coffee." Ardyce poured out three cups of hot coffee as Lucy brought a plate of rolls to the table.

"I see your license plates are from Michigan. So what brings you to Wisconsin?" Lucy inquired.

I told her the story of the deed and the journey. "All we need to do now is find the property," I said.

Looking at the plat map, Mrs. Baxter smiled and told us, "You only have ten miles to go. Head west two miles, turn right on wolf creek road, go another eight miles and turn in to the drive with a rusty blue mailbox out front."

Out of curiosity, I asked, "Did you know the family that originally owned the place?"

Shaking her head, she said, "I only know where the property is because my brother Herman was the mail carrier out the way."

Thanking her for the food and information, we drove west out of Merrill.

CHAPTER NINE

The blue mailbox was leaning to the right as we turned up the rutted drive. I stopped the van and looked around. The log home was a story and a half and seemed to be in good shape. The barn was like none I had ever seen. It was longer, wider and twice the size of the house. The long grass and weeds had taken over the yard. Two oak trees that stood in front of the house desperately needed trimming. Ardyce and I slowly got out of the van and walked around the house to check it out. The sight that greeted us set us back, and we both gasped in surprise!

Rows and rows of trees. An apple orchard! Nothing was mentioned about this in the deed. In a hushed voice of wonder

Ardyce breathed, There must be over a hundred apple trees!" The trees all needed pruning and all hung heavy with fruit. From what I could tell, there were three or four different varieties.

Squeezing my arm, Ardyce said, "Let's look at the house first, then the barn."

I unlocked the heavy oak front door, and we stepped inside. The floor was lightly colored maple. A fieldstone

30

fireplace took up half of the right side wall. To the left was a dining area with a kitchen behind it. The ceiling was open halfway across with a loft area beyond. Beneath the loft were two rooms. The doors were open, and a roll-top desk with a swivel chair was visible against the wall in one room. The other appeared to be empty. No other furniture was visible except for the kitchen where a small table and two chairs sat.

Off the kitchen was a door leading to the cellar. Stepping carefully down the dimly lit stairs, I noticed a light coming from two narrow windows. The walls and floor were fieldstone.

Against the near wall were rows of shelves with four wooden storage bins beneath. In the center of the floor sat a huge furnace, and against the far wall, a stack of firewood. This was beyond our wildest imagination!

Our steps echoed along with the occasional "Oh my" and "Can you believe this?" from Ardyce as we walked through the empty house. The honking of a horn broke us out of our trance. Looking out the open front door, I saw a tall thin man and a stout woman getting out of a pick-up truck. "We have company sweetheart," I called to Ardyce.

The man leaned against the fender of his Model T truck, one hand in the bib of his overalls, the other holding a pipe. The woman stood beside him with her hands in her apron. Ardyce and I walked up, and I held out my hand.

"I'm Aaron Stroud, and this is my wife, Ardyce."

Shaking my hand, the man replied, "I'm Jacob Teeters, just call me Jake, this is my wife, Lilly. Are you folks the new owners?"

"I guess we are," I said. "I found the deed in my father's personal belongings after he died. Do you know when he bought it?"

Taking a puff on his pipe, Jake mused. "It went up for sale five years ago, but the sign came down after a year, so he must have purchased it in the spring of '25. Haven't seen anybody here looking at it in all that time so he must have bought it sight unseen."

"How did you know we were here?" Ardyce asked.

Pointing over my shoulder with his pipe, Jake said, "I was out cultivating corn with Ned when I saw you drive in. Ned is my horse, always use him to cultivate. Went back to the house and got Lilly; told her we ought to find out if we had new neighbors."

His wife stepped forward, took Ardyce by the hand saying, "If you folks would like, I just made some iced tea. Come over to the house and sit a spell. We can tell you all about the old German who used to own this place."

CHAPTER TEN

Sitting on the Teeters front porch sipping iced tea, we heard the most remarkable story of Dieter Grundvall. I got the sense that Jake was a natural-born storyteller. He sipped his ice tea, set it down, lit his pipe and began.

"Dieter and his wife Magda got here back in 1885 and homesteaded the 40 acres. He plowed up the land and started planting apple trees. The first year he put in twenty and every year he added to it."

"How many trees are there now?" asked Ardyce.

"At last count, there were 80 trees," Jake said. "All different varieties. There's Granny Smiths, Golden Delicious, Somerset, and Mcintosh."

"Did he make a living selling apples?" I asked.

With a chuckle, Jake pointed his pipe at me and said, "No sir, he made a living selling cider!"

Then it dawned on me! "That isn't just a barn. It's a barn and a cider mill!"

"That man made the best apple cider I ever tasted. People came from miles around to buy his cider," Lilly said.

"Not just soft cider but the best hard cider in these parts," Jake added, with a smile.

"Did they have any children?" Ardyce asked.

With a sad look, Lilly sighed, "They had two boys. The oldest, Einar, was killed in the great war, and Hans, three years younger, died during the Spanish flu outbreak."

"What happened to make them sell the land?" I wondered.

"Oh, they didn't sell, no sir," Jake spoke up. "About a year after Hans died, Madga got sick with cancer, and six months later she was gone. Dieter tried to run the business by himself, but it proved too much for him. One morning, about six years ago, the mailman found him lying in the front yard dead of a stroke."

Realizing his pipe had gone out, Jake tapped the ash out and began re-packing it. As he worked, he continued, "There wasn't nobody to inherit the property, so the county took it over. Not realizing what they had, they sold it for farmland price. Your Dad probably didn't even know he bought an orchard."

Back at the house, we decided to unpack the van and spend the night indoors. The mattress and bedding went on the floor in the loft; the food and pots and pans took up the kitchen table; the big Blue Bird cookstove looked in good shape. "If you get firewood and some water from the pump and I'll make some coffee, "Ardyce offered.

A small stack of firewood leaned against the side of the barn. I took an armload of the better pieces to the kitchen. Ardyce had learned to cook on a woodstove, so she was right at home. Soon the smell of coffee filled the kitchen. Sitting down across from each other at the small table, I knew the same thought was running through both our minds.

Starting slowly, I said, "I really love this house."

Leaning forward Ardyce replied, "I want to stay here, I mean at least for the summer, and then see if we could live here."

"We will need to find furniture and really explore the possibilities of a life here," I said.

"The first thing we have to do is give this place a good cleaning." Ardyce answered, "and that means a trip into town for a broom, a mop, soap, cleaning rags and curtains for the windows."

I got a pencil and paper from the van, and we began making a list.

CHAPTER ELEVEN

House cleaning in the middle of July is no way to spend a honeymoon. Jake and Lilly had taken a Saturday off to help us get the place in shape. With all the windows open, I could hear the two women talking and laughing as Jake and I worked on clearing out the tall grass in the front yard.

With a scythe, Jake was making real progress. I used a swing blade, and my shoulder would pay for it in the morning. Taking a break to gather up the cuttings, I asked Jake, "What happened to all the furniture?"

Shaking his head in disgust, Jake said, "Some young fella from the tax office decided to pay the tax bill by selling off all the furniture. Old Charlie Grimm bought the bed, but it was too big for their bedroom, so it's sitting in his hayloft. I'll bet you could buy it off him pretty cheap."

"Ardyce," I hollered. "I'll be back in a half-hour."

"Where are you going," she hollered back.

"Going to get us a bed!"

Purchasing the bed cost ten dollars. It was carved oak and worth three times as much, but Charlie was glad to get rid of it. Loading it on Jake's pickup, we took it home and set it up in the loft. Now, we needed a mattress. That meant a trip to Merrill.

"We'll need sheets and blankets too," Ardyce reminded me.

"Maybe you and Lilly should make this trip." I said, "Jake and I want to take a look at the cider mill."

There were two entrances. The double doors to the right were to the barn, the two doors on the left side were to the cider mill.

"Dieter built the barn first, then added the cider mill," Jake explained.

Sliding the doors back on their tracks, we stepped inside. Everything was covered in tarpaulins. Rolling them off slowly, I got my first look at Dieter's apple grinder and press. Jake patted the press like it was an old friend.

"I used to help Dieter during the harvest," he said. "My job was clearing out the strainer."

"Tell me how this thing works," I said.

Pointing with his pipe, Jake walked me through the whole process. "Different types of apples get ripe at different times. The pickers start in late August and go till October. Apples arrive in baskets and are dumped into the grinder." He pointed at the tallest piece of machinery with a hand crank on each side. "It's the toughest job in making cider. Usually, two men worked the grinder, turning the apples into a sauce. The sauce goes down into the strainer, which removes anything that don't belong—like stems or seeds."

Realizing his pipe had gone out again, he popped a wooden match with his thumbnail, got the tobacco burning and continued. "From the strainer, the sauce goes into the press. When the press is full, the lid is dropped, and the handle inserted into the auger. The sauce is pressed until the cider starts running into the vat. From the vat, the cider goes into gallon jars sealed with a cork." Jake pointed to the left wall where wooden boxes were stacked under another tarp. Against the back wall was a stack of about 50 wooden barrels.

Scratching my head, I asked, "How many people does this whole operation take?"

Jake puffed on his pipe a few times and then said, "Dieter used to hire folks from Merrill to do the picking. Otherwise, it was him, Magda and the two boys along with me and Lilly and our son Elmer. Elmer and his wife June have a place two miles down the road from us. Our daughter Francine is at that teacher college in Oshkosh."

I got the feeling I would get Jake's life story in bits and pieces.

CHAPTER TWELVE

The barn held a few more surprises. All the horse stalls had been taken out to make room for the 1921 REO flatbed truck! Taking off his hat, scratching his head and giving a low whistle, Jake said, "By golly, I forgot about this old truck! Dieter bought it new to haul the apples from the field." It seemed in good shape, except the tires were flat.

"I wonder how that tax man missed this?" Jake murmured looking through the window. The field mice had nibbled at the leather seats. I then opened the side panel to check the motor. Probably needed new belts and hoses, but that shouldn't cost too much.

"Billy Dehn at the garage in Merrill could have this running for you with a day's work," Jake said.

"How many bushels of apples did you get per tree?" I asked.

The cider expert educated me. Tipping his hat back with his thumb, Jake said, "Dieter got between 12 and 15 bushels per tree, depending on the variety. One bushel of apples can give you about 5 gallons of cider, so you get maybe 70 gallons per tree."

My mind was spinning! "That's over 5,000 gallons of cider, where would I put it all!"

Jake started laughing so hard he almost fell over. "When folks find out you are making cider, you could be selling one hundred gallons a day, at three dollars a gallon, and most will bring their own jugs!"

Lilly and Ardyce drove into the yard with a new mattress covered in brown paper and tied with twine. Jake and I hefted the mattress up to the loft while the women brought in the sheets, pillows, blankets and of all things, a chamber pot!

After Jake and Lilly left, I sat Ardyce down at the kitchen table and told her the whole story about the cider press, the truck, and everything else. She looked stunned at first, then her eyes lit up, and a big smile spread across her pretty face.

"I wondered how we could make a living here," she said excitedly. "Now we know. We make and sell cider!" Then her brow furrowed. "Aaron, what about prohibition? Making and selling any alcohol is against the law."

"Jake explained that to me. What we turn out is *soft cider*, no alcohol in it. Of course, if people buy it and let it sit on a shelf for two months to ferment, well, then it turns itself into hard cider," I said, and then smiled.

That night, as we lay in bed, we began making plans. "We have about a month and a half before the first apples are ready to pick, and our money is running low," I said softly.

Like she was reading my mind, Ardyce sat up and said, "I can take the train from Merrill back to Lansing. I will tell my parents all about the apples and the cider mill and get the money from the bank." The moonlight through the window framed her lovely face.

"While you are gone, I'll get the truck running, get the grinder and press-ready and have a telephone installed."

"Have the electric company put in power and some lights too," she said.

CHAPTER THIRTEEN

The train rolled out of the Merrill station with Ardyce waving from a Pullman car window. It was the first time we had really been apart, and I was already missing her. I drove to the garage and talked to Billy Dehn.

"I can be out tomorrow, and I'll bring some tires along just in case we need them," he said.

Next stop was the telephone company. They said someone would be there in two or three days.

The electric company was next. "I'll have our guy come out this afternoon to see what needs to be done," the supervisor said.

Driving home, I prayed the money I had left would last until Ardyce got back.

I took my first long walk through the orchard. The trees were loaded with green apples. At the back end of the property was a woodlot, about five acres of pines, birches, and hardwoods. We needed firewood now and for the coming winter. Thank God we had a source. Now, I just needed to get it cut and hauled home. Walking back to the house, I could see most of the apple trees needed pruning. The growth needed to go to the apples, not more branches.

Billy Dehn had his work cut out for him, but he seemed to enjoy it. Crawling out from under the motor, he said, "You need a new fan belt and radiator hose. Them mice have been real busy. I'll change the oil and put in some new plugs. The tires are shot, but I got some good used ones I brought along that should do fine." I could almost feel the bills fading from my wallet.

"Can you give me a rough estimate of how much this will cost?" I asked.

He tugged at his left ear, which left an oil smudge and said, "With the used tires I can do the job for $35."

The telephone went on the wall in the kitchen. The good news was the installation charge went on the first month's bill. The telephone company had to dig a hole by the road, set in a pole then run the line to the house. Fortunately, the electric company could use the same pole. A wall outlet in every room with an overhead light in the kitchen, the loft, the office, the spare room, and two lights hanging from the rafters in the cellar. Again, the installation charge would be on the bill. *Hurry home, Ardyce. Please hurry home.*

I finally met Jake's son Elmer. I was having morning coffee when they parked in the drive. Elmer was as tall as his dad but more massive across the shoulders with a head of sandy hair.

"So, you're going to be the new cider maker," Elmer said with a grin.

"With a little help and a lot of luck," I said.

"Me and Luther Hobart always took turns on the grinder, and we are ready to do it again," Elmer said.

"You need some firewood?" Jake said. "If Billy got that REO running, let's go cut a few cords." Loading saws and axes on the truck we drove to the woodlot.

There were plenty of downed trees ready to be cut. Jake lopped off the branches while Elmer and I worked the two-person saw. Oak, ash, and birch with some pine made a good load.

Stopping for sandwiches and iced tea that Lilly bought over, Jake said, "Old Cyrus Spranger and his wife are selling out and moving to Arizona. Their son works for the Indian bureau there. They got a dining room table and chairs to get rid of, probably get it for a good price."

"Sure beats cutting wood, I'll go with you," offered Elmer.

CHAPTER FOURTEEN

The dining room table came with two leaves and six chairs—slightly nicked and dinged after years of use. Looking around, I could see most of the other furniture was gone.

"We are leaving first of August," Cyrus drawled. "So, I'll make you a package deal. I've got a two-year-old Kelvinator washing machine to sell too. I'll take $50, and it's all yours."

I glanced at Elmer, who gave a slight nod of his head. "You got a deal," I said, and we shook hands.

I ate supper that night with Jake and Lilly. While we were having coffee, the telephone jangled. Lilly answered, talked a minute, then held out the receiver. "Would you like to say hello to your wife?" she asked me.

I almost tipped my chair over getting to the phone. "I love you. when are you coming home?"

I could hear her laughter, then she said, "I will be on the afternoon train Saturday. Have you missed me?"

"Terribly, and I'm down to our last seven dollars. I've got some surprises waiting for you."

"I hope they are nice surprises. I have one for you too."

She looked more beautiful than when she had left. Ardyce stepped off the train and right into my arms. The kiss lasted long enough for people to start clapping.

Holding me close, she whispered, "Let's go home." I loaded four suitcases in the van. She had packed all of her clothes, and it looked like all of mine. She laid her hand on my shoulder as I drove.

"So what surprise do you have for me?" I asked.

"The morning after I got back to Lansing, I wasn't feeling well. Of course, Mom took me to her doctor. I guess I wasn't too surprised to find out I'm pregnant."

I almost drove off the road! I managed to pull over and stop. Ardyce sat there, smiling. "How's that for a surprise?"

I hugged her as tears leaked from the corner of my eyes. I was going to be a father! "When is this surprise coming?"

"Not until April, so we have plenty of time to plan," she said.

"I hope you like what I've done with the place," I said, opening the front door.

She slid her hand across the dining table. "It's just what we needed." As she stepped into the kitchen, I flipped the switch, and the overhead light came on. In the corner sat the washing machine. With a gasp of joy, she turned the rollers and lifted the cover.

"I was going to plead with you to get me one of these and here it is!" Then the telephone caught her eye. "I'll have to call my folks later and let them know I'm home, "She said.

"The not-so-good news is we are down to twelve dollars." I hated to spoil the moment.

"Actually my dear, we have *three thousand* and twelve dollars," she said with a big smile. Untucking her blouse, she untied a brown bow at her waist and removed out a slightly bulky sash.

Laying it on the kitchen table, she explained, "The money belt was Mom's idea. There are three pockets with ten one hundred dollar bills in each one."

"This will be our operating capital," I said. "And I hope and pray it will be enough."

CHAPTER FIFTEEN

The heat of July gave way to the heat of August. As I helped Jake and Elmer put up another crop of hay, Ardyce got a lesson in canning vegetables with June and Lilly. June and Elmer had one child, a girl named Louise who was three and into everything. All-in-all, it was a great summer.

We had already washed down and checked over the grinder and press. "Every year when the cider was done, Dieter spent days cleaning and checking everything," Jake informed me. "So, you shouldn't have any trouble when the picking starts."

Back in the woodlot, Elmer showed me a big patch of blackberries. When they ripened, we picked pails full. "June makes the best blackberry jam I ever tasted. If we split the berries, I'll have her make you some." Grinning to myself, I realized how well neighbors took care of each other out here. When you helped with the work, you reaped the rewards.

Big cobs of sweet corn fresh from the stalk are like a gift from the Almighty. As Ardyce and I worked our way through a steaming plateful, she dropped a few more pearls of wisdom on me.

"Lilly told me when we start selling the cider, we should

trade for as much produce as we can to see us through the winter."

"Did she mention anything in particular?" I asked.

"Potatoes, carrots, cabbage, and onions. That's what the bins in the cellar are for." Thinking this made a great deal of sense, I nodded my head.

"How about canned stuff, can we trade for those?"

"We can, but we have to be careful. Some people don't take the care they should when canning, but Lilly will take care of that," she answered smugly.

"I think next year we should plant a garden," I said.

"And I'll also need canning jars, lids, wax and a pressure cooker like Lilly has," was the answer.

"That *will* be a lot of work for a new mother."

"I'll be fine. I will have all the help I need," she said with a big smile.

We drove into Merrill for two reasons. I placed an ad in the Merrill Herald paper for apple pickers to start in one week. I offered a campsite for out-of-towners and a decent wage. The second reason was check-up for Ardyce at a doctor recommended by Lilly and June, who said everything was fine and for Ardyce to come back in two months.

We stopped for groceries at the market and went to the bank to change some of the hundred dollar bills into fives, tens, and twenties.

"We're going to need some baby supplies soon," I said.

She patted my arm softly. "I already know what we'll need, and we can get those things later. We may need the money for other things right now."

That evening there was a light breeze as we walked through the orchard. Jake had pointed out where we needed to start picking. The trees bowed under the weight of the fruit. *Am I ready for this?* Anything could happen. The truck could break down, the grinder could lose a gear, the press could break and what if no pickers showed up? What seemed like an easy moneymaker could turn around and bite me in the backside. It was a gamble, but then so was everything. A few extra prayers tonight couldn't hurt.

As we lay in bed, I asked Ardyce, "Do you think Dad knew about any of this?"

"I very much doubt he did. What would he have done if he had found it waiting for him?"

With a smile, I held her hand and said, "He would have done exactly what we're doing. He would have looked forward to the challenge and carried it through."

Turning on her side and snuggling close, Ardyce whispered, "Like father, like son."

CHAPTER SIXTEEN

"Me and Elmer is ready," said Luther Hobart. All six-foot of him was muscle. His big weather-beaten hands looked as if they could crush rock. His shaggy mop of dark hair topped a smile that went from ear to ear.

Ardyce was driving the REO truck bringing in the first load of apples. Pickers arrived during the night and set up camp. About two dozen men and women were in the orchard filling the bushel baskets and loading them on the flatbed. As they came off the truck, more hands dumped the apples into pails and carried them to the grinder.

A middle-aged woman with short hair and arm muscles that matched mine brought the pails to the grinder and with a nod from Elmer, dumped one in. The grinder had a big handle on each side, one for Luther, one for Elmer. With a slow, steady movement, the apples disappeared, to be replaced by more apples. The aroma was sharp and tangy.

The sauce ran down into the strainer where Jake stirred it with a long paddle. About every two hours, the strainer had to be emptied into a barrel and rinsed with water. The pure sauce went to the press. When enough sauce filled the press, two men on top would turn the auger, lowering the lid. What ran out of the press was *not* apple juice. It was cloudy with sediment and tart to the taste.

Three women filled the jugs that were standing ready. One turned the spigot, one held the bottle, and one corked the full jugs. The jugs were placed on the shelves that had been cleaned the week before in preparation.

I got a little nervous when the sheriff's car drove into the yard. I waited until he got out of the car and then walked to the vehicle. Then I heard a voice behind me holler over the noise, "Hi Dad, we're making cider!" It was Luther with a big smile, waving.

"Putting out his hand, the sheriff said, "Nice to meet you, Mr. Stroud, I'm Melvin Hobart. That's my son on the grinder. When he told me the cider mill was back in business, I knew I had to meet you."

He was built just like Luther, but middle age had given him a spare tire around his waist and a sprinkling of gray in his dark hair.

"Nice to meet you, sir, it's good of you to stop by," I said.

"Have you tasted any of the first cider yet?" he asked. An opportunity like this was not to be passed up.

"My opinion of the flavor would tend to be a little biased," I said. "Would you do me the honor of giving me an honest opinion?"

"It would be my pleasure," Taking a glass from the shelf, I handed it to the woman at the spigot. She carefully filled it and handed it to Melvin.

He took a slow sip at first, rolling it on his tongue, then quickly drained the glass. Smacking his lips, he reached for his wallet. "I may be your first customer, but certainly not the last. That's as good as Dieter's if not better. I'll take three jugs, and I'll have my deputies spread the word you are open for business."

That evening, after supper, Ardyce and I drove to Baxter's Motor Court. Mrs. Baxter was sitting on the porch when we arrived.

"It's my young couple from Lansing. I heard you re-opened the cider mill." I handed her a jug of cider.

"I have a business deal for you if you are a cider drinker. If you let folks know we are open, there will be more of these in the future." She accepted the jug with a smile and a nod.

"I would do it without the cider, but this just makes it a sweet deal."

As September reached the half-way date, the cider making had settled into a daily rhythm. Everyone knew their job and did it well. I talked Ardyce into letting an older woman, named Mildred, drive the flatbed.

CHAPTER SEVENTEEN

Jake was right about the cider. People showed up to buy every afternoon. Lilly traded for produce and canned goods, and still, the money came in. From as far south as Wausau and as far north as Rhinelander, customers waited in line for cider. When the cellar bins were full, we nailed a sign to the pole by the road, CASH ONLY. By the end of each day, there were seldom more than a dozen jugs of cider on the shelves. Many bought their own jugs to be filled.

The pickers were paid every Saturday at noon when we stopped work. Some opted to be half cash, half cider. Saturday afternoons were for cleanup. We ran water through everything, a suggestion from Jake. "You don't want that sticky juice building up in there. You gotta flush it out," he said, wisely.

Elmer and June got paid every week, but Jake and Lilly wanted to wait until the end of the season. "What you don't got yet, you don't spend yet," according to Jake.

The strainer barrel was three-quarters full. As I was scratching my head wondering what to do with it, Jake ambled up and solved the problem.

"Butch and Tony Jenske are coming to get that barrel. They run a pig farm north of here. They'll give you five dollars for it and bring back the barrel." Of course! Jake probably already knew it, but he had just added to his bonus at the end of the season.

The shiny new Packard seemed out of place as it parked in the yard. Two men in suits got out and looked around. The driver was lean and tanned with a small mustache. The passenger was an older portly man with a cane and a slight limp. I walked toward them and held out my hand.

"I'm Aaron Stroud, how can I help you?"

"I am Devon Blake, and it is a pleasure to meet you," the portly man said with a smile. "I own the finest restaurant in Merrill, and I have been getting some requests for your cider from my patrons."

Sensing an opportunity, I asked, "Can you estimate how much cider will be needed?"

"I believe 25 to 30 gallons per week. Can you supply that much?"

"I am sure we can meet your needs. It will cost four dollars per gallon, in cash, delivered every Friday until the season ends in October."

Nodding his head, Mr. Blake remarked, "I like the way you do business, Mr. Stroud. Let's start with 25 gallons and proceed from there."

September slipped slowly in October. The nights were cooler, and the humidity disappeared. Ardyce slowed down some as the new life inside her grew. Her second checkup showed everything as it should be.

"I need a sewing machine," she told me one evening.

I had learned never to ask why she needed something. Like a well-trained husband, I asked, "When and what kind?"

The next morning I returned from Merrill with a Singer treadle sewing machine and a box of thread. We still had no living room furniture. We decided to wait until the cider making was over and buy some new chairs and a sofa. We also decided to turn the old office into a bathroom in the coming spring.

Ardyce kept her parents up-to-date on everything with a telephone call every Saturday.

"We need to set some of those bushels of apples out front. Folks will be canning and making applesauce," Jake informed me one morning. That day we sold five bushels. I listened to everything Jake told me and he had yet to be wrong. I was learning the apple business on a day-to-day basis.

Lilly took Ardyce through the making of her first apple pie. It didn't last two days—it was that good. I hoped there were more to come. She had always been a good cook, and now she was a baker as well.

CHAPTER EIGHTEEN

By the third week of October, I thought the demand for cider would ease up. Instead, it increased. "Holidays are coming up, folks are getting ready," was Jake's opinion.

I had set a jug of cider in the cellar wanting to find out for myself what hard cider tasted like. My idea was to celebrate with Jake and Elmer when the cider season was over.

One day, I watched the pickers come in from the orchard walking behind the REO flatbed and then looked at the calendar on the wall—October 28, 1929. The apples were unloaded, some went out front, most went to the grinder.

"Last batch Mr. Stroud," yelled Luther. He was eating an apple with one hand and turning the crank with the other. I made a silent vow never to arm wrestle Luther.

I paid off the pickers and gave each one a five-dollar bonus. Some opted to stay a few more days to help with the last of the cider and the cleanup. There were only 18 jugs of cider on the shelves and none in the barrels. The final delivery to the Blake restaurant would be tomorrow—October 29, 1929.

The daily cleanup was almost done when the Model T slowly drove in. Jake gave it a hard look and mumbled, "Be back in a minute."

Two young men got out of the Ford, looked all around, and slowly walked up to the open doors.

"Got any cider left," one of them asked.

"How many do you want?" I inquired. Reaching into his back jeans pocket, he came out with a slim Colt pistol. The other man just stood there waiting.

"How about you keep the cider and just hand over the money," he said, pointing the gun at me.

"I don't carry much on me," I told him.

"You been raking in cash with this cider, now hand it over," he snarled.

From the corner of my eye, I saw a long shadow appear behind him. Then I heard CLACK, CLACK, the unmistakable sound of a pump shotgun.

"If you two want to get out of this alive, drop the pistol." It was Jake! He must have known there was something not right about them when they drove in. He had gone to the house and gotten my .12 gauge Winchester. He poked the man with the gun in the back with the barrel of the shotgun.

"I won't tell you again, drop it!" Realizing he might be going to die, the man wisely dropped the gun. "Ardyce already called the Sheriff, he should be here soon," Jake let me know.

Jake had them lying face down in the yard when Sheriff Hobart came rolling in. He handcuffed them then turned them over.

"Tommy Lamont and Grover Spruell," he snorted. "Two of the troublemakers from Merrill." I went to hand him the Colt I had picked up, but he waved his hand.

"You keep that as a souvenir. You might even want to keep it close, just in case." We loaded the two hoodlums in the back of his car, and he headed back to town.

Jake handed me the shotgun, pulled out his pipe, and lit it.

"How did you know they were up to no good?" I asked. Jake took a deep puff and pointed the pipe at me.

"I saw when they drove in they weren't smiling. People coming to get cider always smile."

Ardyce came out of the house to make sure we were alright. After giving us both a hug, I asked her to take the shotgun back to the house. I racked the pump back to empty out the shells, but I need not have bothered. It was empty!

I just stared at Jake, who explained, "Didn't have time to find the shells, so I just kinda played it by ear."

We found out later that both men were on the run from holding up a gas station in Tomahawk. They had planned on working their way south and spending all their money on a good time in Milwaukee. Instead, they each got a five-year sentence in the Green Bay prison.

CHAPTER NINETEEN

Tuesday morning, I left Jake, Elmer, and Luther to clean up while I delivered the last cider to Blake's Restaurant. The cook's helper and I unloaded the cider and carried it into the pantry. The cook handed me an envelope with the payment.

Next stop was the bank to change some bills. I couldn't even get close. There was a crowd that blocked the sidewalk and spilled out into the street. Getting out of the van, I asked a man in a butcher's apron what was going on.

"Ain't you heard? That stock market in New York crashed! If you got any money in here, you better get it out before they close. Otherwise, it'll be gone!"

Not making the connection, I asked, "How can that be?"

The butcher explained, "All these banks have been buying up stock shares on the cuff. Now the market wants the money, and the banks want to give them ours, so we have to get it first."

Very quietly, I got in the van and drove home.

Ardyce was on the telephone with her mother when I walked in the door.

Hanging up the receiver, she asked, "Have you heard about the banks?"

I explained what the butcher had said. "I know your dad had money invested in the market, will he be able to get through this panic?"

"Mom is afraid they could lose everything, including the Ford dealership." I could hear the worry and fear in her voice.

"As long as they have enough money for train fare they will always have a home here," I said.

"My place is paid off, but Elmer still owes on his," Jake told me. The cider mill was cleaned and covered with tarps. Elmer sat on a stool, looking pale.

"If I can find enough work to get through the winter, I should be in good shape," Elmer said.

Stroking my chin, I asked, "Who does the snow plowing around here in the winter?"

"The county only plows the roads, everybody else either does their own or hires it done if they can find someone with a plow, which there ain't many of," Jake said.

"OK, here's the deal, "I spoke firmly. "We still have wood to cut for winter. After that, we can find a plow for the REO. Elmer runs the plow. Start asking around for customers, maybe get a regular route going, but I get plowed out first."

Elmer looked like I had thrown him a lifeline. Jake just nodded his head like it was the natural solution.

That night after supper Ardyce and I counted the money in the cashbox. We were both stunned to find out we had $7,520.

"I haven't paid Jake, yet. I plan to give him and Lilly $500. Without them helping us, we wouldn't have made all this." Patting my hand and smiling, Ardyce said, "That's a wonderful idea, how much cider is left to sell?"

"There are about 22 jugs on the shelves yet. Let's keep two and sell the rest to Blake's Restaurant. If we watch our expenses, this winter we will be in good shape."

CHAPTER TWENTY

Slowly, the enormity of the market crash was settling in in northern Wisconsin. Small businesses were the first to go. Then as the money supply dried up the larger businesses were forced to close their doors. Factories shut down, throwing hundreds out of work. People left to find refuge with families elsewhere who were also out of work. Banks began calling in mortgages and foreclosing on farms.

Ardyce and I were able to buy a new living room set, which normally sold for $225. When the store went out of business, we paid $50 for a sofa, two chairs, two end tables, and a coffee table. New tires for the REO cost $25.

After the carnage was over, only two banks in Merrill remained open. The other four locked the doors, boarded up the windows, and moved on. Not one auto dealership made it. In places, the city looked like a ghost town.

We found a used snow plow blade for the truck in Tomahawk for $20. Elmer would be in business. A week before Thanksgiving, Jake, Elmer and I butchered a cow. I had field-dressed deer, so I was actually a help.

Thanksgiving was at Jake and Lilly's house with a beef roast, potatoes, green beans, candied carrots, homemade biscuits and two pies—apple and blackberry. As we sat and talked over coffee later, Elmer told us he had eight customers lined up to plow.

"It'll be January and February that will be the tough months," he said. They are the coldest and snowiest."

I hoped and prayed the worst of the crash was over. It wasn't.

Ardyce's parents, Bernard and Eunice, were able to take the train from Lansing and spend Christmas with us. Unlike many of those in Lansing, Bernard Johnson did not panic. Having been a member of the Democratic party for years, Bernard turned to those in power and offered his help. He did lose the Ford dealership but kept his house. He was helping to organize the Michigan Civilian Conservation Corps. He now worked for the Federal Government. His income was secure. Like a cat, Bernard had landed on his feet.

He and Eunice were fascinated by the cider mill. On Christmas Eve I broke out the hard cider to celebrate. It was better than fine wine. Even Eunice got a little tipsy.

Ardyce was in her sixth month of pregnancy and more beautiful than ever. The tree was a little short on decorations, so we made many of our own. As we sat before the fire in the big fireplace, we talked of memories and future plans. The one picture I had of Dad was the one from our wedding. Ardyce had it framed, and it was on the mantle. Reuben was with us, as he would always be.

January 1930 started with a blizzard. It raged for two days dumping eighteen inches of snow across northern Wisconsin. Elmer had more work than one man could handle. Jake spelled him on the plow for six hours while he warmed up.

The big furnace in our cellar kept the house warm and inviting. The REO truck just took it all in stride, running like a champ.

One cold February morning, I received a call from the train station.

"Mr. Stroud, we have a parcel for you to pick up," the baggage manager told me.

I started the van and drove into Merrill. A large wooden crate awaited me; the label said it was from Bernard Johnson in Lansing, Michigan. It just fit in the van. When I got it home, Ardyce helped me unpack it. Inside was a cradle!

"Dad told me they were going to send a gift for the baby," Ardyce said. "This is just what we need!" We had a crib set up in the loft, but during the day this would be perfect for the living room.

The radio in the kitchen kept us informed about the aftermath of the market crash. Soup kitchens and homeless shelters were overwhelmed with families trying to make it through the winter. Merrill opened the abandoned furniture store to shelter and feed hundreds. Trucks from Milwaukee brought in surplus food and blankets. The price of everything plummeted. America was floundering its way through a living nightmare.

March arrived with more snow. Not a blizzard, just a steady snowfall for 24 hours. The REO was becoming a familiar sight to the local farmers. Elmer's route kept the wolf from his door and the bank off his back. Those without money paid him in whatever they had to offer—smoked hams, eggs by the dozen, dressed chickens, and an occasional quarter of venison. Ardyce made a venison stew. I ate until I could hold no more. The baby was giving out a kick now and then, let us know he would soon be ready.

CHAPTER TWENTY-ONE

The baby arrived with the first robins of April. Ardyce had begun labor pains about mid-morning. We made it to the hospital in Merrill in plenty of time. She was calm and ready. I was a nervous wreck. Two hours later, a nurse came out.

"Mr. Stroud, everything went fine. Come see your new son."

Ardyce was holding the tiniest human I had ever seen. "Aaron, meet your son Reuben," she said with a tired smile.

I was afraid to hold the baby. What if I dropped it or held it wrong? I guess the nurse had been through this many times. She tenderly placed the infant in my arms, showing me how to rock it gently. I was a father!

Sometimes alone, sometimes in pairs, they came walking down Wolf Creek road looking for work, any work that could earn money or just a little food. I found jobs for as many as I could. They cleaned the barn and the cider mill. They planted flowers and split wood. Some walked the orchard, picking up the branches that had fallen over the winter. We gave them food and housed them overnight in the barn. Ardyce mended their clothes on the sewing machine. They would move on to be replaced by others. None left hungry or broke, all left feeling just a little better about themselves.

"This old truck saved my farm," Elmer told me as we took the snowplow off in the barn. He had been able to make the mortgage payments all winter, and the bank was happy not to have to carry another farm they couldn't sell.

Little Reuben was a joy. He was not a screamer or a squaller, just an occasional holler to let you know he needed changing or feeding. Lilly and June stopped by almost daily with a trinket or booties or just to hold and talk to him. Whatever was on the spoon in his mouth, he ate. The clothesline always had at least a half-dozen diapers drying. The singer sewing machine got a real workout. The kid had more clothes than Ardyce and I put together.

The one gift that was unexpected but welcome came from Luther Hobart. He drove up one day, parked and got a box from the car.

"Me and Dad got Reuben a playmate," he said with his big smile. Setting the box down, he lifted out a Golden Labrador puppy. "His name is Sam. He and Reuben can grow up together and be best friends."

Luther was right; the two little ones bonded immediately. They played together, napped together and got in trouble together just as nature intended.

The apple trees blossomed in May. The aroma of the new blossoms was intoxicating. Elmer and I had pruned the trees in the fall, taking out suckers and old branches, trading the Applewood to the Jenske brothers who used it to smoke their hams. He provided us with a smoked ham at Easter. It seemed the Teeter family had adopted Ardyce and me into the family. It was a comforting feeling.

I had promised Ardyce a bathroom. I contracted the work to Castor Brothers Plumbing from Tomahawk on Jake's recommendation. Avril and Willie Castor both showed up the second week in May and took charge of the project. What had been the office would now have indoor plumbing.

Ardyce chose a bathtub and a sink from pictures in a book of fixtures. She also wanted a faucet in the kitchen to replace the hand pump. A new well was dug, a drainage field laid out and a trench dug to bring the water up through the basement. Looking at the fieldstone wall, I did not even want to know how they would bring pipe through. It took a month to complete at a cost of $350. It was worth every penny. The year before the same work would have cost us three times as much.

We expanded the campsite to include shower areas and two more outhouses. Rocks were hauled in for fire pits, and clotheslines strung out. Many of these pickers would be families on the move with children. We built a fenced-in play area with swings and a sandbox. A water barrel was placed at each site. It would be their job to fill it from the pump as needed.

Old Ned kept a slow, steady pace as he pulled the plow. Jake hardly needed the reins he was holding. A half-acre seemed like a lot to me for a garden, but Jake insisted.

"Folks won't be bringing vegetables to trade for cider this year," he told me. "They'll be storing them for themselves."

He was right as usual. Hard times had a chokehold on the entire nation. The price of goods and services were still dropping. I knew the price of cider would have to fall as well, along with the amount paid to the pickers and other workers. Talking it over with Jake, we decided that fifty cents a gallon was fair. I also wrote a letter to our Senator in Madison asking if the Government would be interested in purchasing some cider to dole out at the food kitchens set up across the state. I had not received an answer yet but was hopeful.

CHAPTER TWENTY-TWO

"I'm gonna raise rabbits," Jake told me one day. Lighting his pipe, he explained his new venture. "I can't keep killing off my chickens. I need them for eggs. The rabbits are a good meat source that just keeps supplying itself."

The more I thought about it, the more sense it made. Ardyce agreed, saying, "It's something we should think about doing. We have plenty of room in the barn."

The mail carrier finally delivered some good news. I got a letter back from the Senator in Madison. They were not interested in our cider stating it was not a recommended food source for children. However, the letter read in part, 'When your apple crop is ripe and ready for harvest we would like to purchase as many bushels as you can supply at $5 per bushel. An agent from your area will arrive every Friday to take delivery and issue payment.'

"Make sure you get cash," was Jake's answer. It gave me a good feeling to know that no apples would go to waste.

Much needed rain fell steadily for a day and a half. The garden soaked it up, and everything in it seemed to grow overnight. Green beans, potatoes, corn, cabbage, onions, carrots, lettuce, peas, and rutabaga's all reaching for the sunlight.

We had stocked up on canning supplies in Merrill and bought a pressure cooker for Ardyce.

"I am also going to can rabbit meat," I was told.

Elmer gave us some of the venison June had canned in the fall, and the stew Ardyce made still lived in my memory.

The next morning, I stepped out on the front porch with my morning coffee. Coming down the road was a horse and wagon with two men on the high seat. I waved, and the driver turned into the drive. The horse, the harness, the wagon, and the men had seen better days. As the wagon came to a stop, another man who had been sitting down in the back stood up.

All three looked the same. Tall, about six foot, lean, without being skinny, wearing bib overalls, plaid shirts and old felt hats. Their age was hard to tell, perhaps late forties. The rider got down and walked forward. I met him in the yard and shook his hand.

"I'm Seth Frankel," the man said. "the man driving the team is my brother Abner, the one in the back is my brother Fred. We do roofing and carpenter work. If you got anything that needs fixing, we boys can do it."

Seth and I took a walk around the house and barn. A corner of the porch roof was missing some cedar shakes that had escaped my attention. The barn roof was alright, but there were a few loose boards.

"How much do you charge for your work?" I asked.

72

Cupping his chin with his hand, he thought a minute then said, "I think five dollars ought to cover it." I agreed, and he walked back to the wagon to tell his brothers.

Seth and Abel were patching the porch roof while Fred watched.

Jake arrived in his pickup, got out and strolled over. "I figured the 'we' boys would show up after the rain," he said.

"Do you know these guys?" I asked.

With a chuckle, Jake said, "These boys are local. They tend to show up after some bad weather looking for work. Seth and Abel do most of it. Fred was in the great war, and it never left him. Sometimes he thinks he's still there in the trenches waiting to go over the wall. He's harmless, just keep an eye on him."

By noon the work was done. I paid Seth and the old horse slowly pulled the old wagon down the road.

CHAPTER TWENTY-THREE

One year ago, Ardyce and I arrived at our new home. Many things had changed since then. Little Reuben was four months old and the joy of our life. We had made some changes to the house Dieter Grundvall had built. We had electricity, a telephone, and indoor plumbing. The cider mill was back in business, and the orchard had been trimmed and pruned.

Not all the changes were good. The stock market had crashed, throwing the nation into a depression. Thousands of people were unemployed, and many were homeless. Breadlines and soup kitchens became common sights in every city and town. The price of everything had bottomed out because no one had money to buy. Likewise, the wages paid to those who could find work had fallen. A dollar a day was considered good wages.

The big cities faced a new problem. Prohibition had given rise to bootleg whiskey from Canada and homemade stills turning out corn liquor. Gangs were fighting over who would rule this underworld business.

Farmers were going broke because they were paid almost nothing for milk or crops. They kept farming because it was their only way to stay alive. Almost nothing was better than nothing at all.

Walking the orchard on a hot July morning, it was easy to see the pruning had done its work. Every tree seemed to have twice the apples as last year. The problem I faced was how to balance the amount of cider we produced against the bushels of apples the Government would buy. Would people have the money to buy cider?

"Why not run an advertisement in the Milwaukee papers that we have cider for sale?" Ardyce asked.

"Your wife is a smart lady. Listen to her," was Jake's advice.

I decided to do run the ad the week before picking started.

Ardyce would not be joining us in the cider mill this year. With Reuben to care for, the garden to tend and the house to look after, her hands would be full. With Jake, Elmer, Lilly, June and Luther to help run things, I felt confident everything would work out.

We began getting telephone calls from southeastern Wisconsin asking when we would start making cider. I told them the first week in August and usually ran until the end of October. The standard answer was, "Someone will be there to buy cider."

An ore boat company based in Superior wanted cider for their crews stating it was difficult to keep fresh apples aboard. A restaurant in Lake Geneva promised to have an agent there to buy cider. Just as Ardyce had predicted the ad in the newspaper paid off.

Ardyce remained busy canning her first yield from our garden. Not having used a pressure cooker before, Lilly was there to supervise. June had the toughest job of babysitting Reuben, Sam and her daughter Louise.

Jake and Elmer were running hot water through the grinder just for something to do. The strainer got a new screen, bushel baskets were mended and counted, and the glass jugs were rinsed. Dieter had left us eight bags of corks, five of which we still had. We changed the oil in the REO truck and aired up the tires.

Elmer came out of the barn, wiping his hands on a rag. "Let's go pick some berries," he said with a smile.

"Let's take Jake along," I answered.

With a laugh, Elmer told me, "Dad eats as much as he picks, but it will keep him busy."

The blackberries were plentiful and as big as my thumb. We had brought four lard pails with us, and we filled them all.

"I can taste that blackberry jam already," I told Elmer.

"I'm thinkin' about Lilly's blackberry rhubarb pie," Jake mumbled. I remembered that pie and my mouth started watering.

Nudging his Dad in the ribs, Elmer told him, "Eat less and pick more, and then you may get two pies."

With his mouth full of berries, Jake just nodded his head.

CHAPTER TWENTY-FOUR

The campsites were full, and we had to turn people away. We had hired more than we needed just to give them work. The lady who had driven the truck last year, Mildred, held the same position this year. It was her job to make sure the load was stable on the flatbed so that none fell off on the way to the mill. Her sister Lottie and two friends worked the spigot, filled the bottles and corked them. Elmer and Luther on the grinder, Jake on the strainer and Calvin with his cousin Eugene working the press were all ready for the first load of apples.

Eager hands began reaching for the baskets as the truck drove up to the double doors. "Be careful with those baskets," Mildred hollered. "You damage 'em, and it comes out of your pay!" She looked at me, gave me a wink, and turned back to the unloading. We both knew nobody would have to pay for a damaged basket, but it helped the workers take a little more care.

We filled the first one hundred bottles without selling one. I was getting a bit worried, but we continued making cider. About two o'clock in the afternoon, three shiny new Ford pickup trucks drove in and parked. A tall man wearing tan slacks, a short-sleeved white shirt and a Fedora hat eased out of the first truck and walked over.

As I shook his hand, he said, "I'm John Pickett from Lake Geneva. I called you in July about the cider. Do you have some ready?"

With a smile, I told him, "we have 150 gallons ready, how much would you like?"

"I will take it all. Is there a charge for the jugs?"

"We usually charge 10 cents deposit on each jug," I told him. Nodding his head, he handed me a one hundred dollar bill. I gave him ten dollars in change and told him to have the trucks back up to the door. Fifty jugs per vehicle and then they drove away headed south.

The workers had been watching this, so I held up the bill and yelled, "Let's make cider!" They yelled and clapped their hands, knowing everything would be alright.

More buyers trickled in as the day wore on. It was not the volume or waiting lines of last year, but people still wanted cider. Sheriff Hobart got his two jugs, the District Attorney Gillis Pinkel bought three, and at the end of the day, we only had sixteen jugs left.

Mildred parked the truck and said, "All those bushels and the trees look like we hardly picked any. I've never seen so many apples."

Ardyce and I walked the campsite that evening, getting to know the pickers. Her apron pockets were full of hard candy that she handed out to the children.

The one item most needed was flour to make biscuits or pan bread. I made a note to get two 50 lb. bags of flour from Merrill tomorrow. The campsites were orderly, and the pickers seemed happy to have work.

Friday afternoon, a bright yellow Mack 'bulldog' truck came slowly down Wolf Creek Road and turned into the yard. A heavyset man with a clipboard got down from the passenger seat and walked to the double doors of the cider mill. Holding out his hand, he said, "I'm Cecil Andrews, I'm here to pick up some apples for the Government food program."

With a firm handshake, I replied, "We have been expecting you." Pointing to the bushel baskets sitting in the shade of the oak tree in the yard. "I have fifty bushels ready to go."

We walked over to the tree where he began writing on his clipboard. Picking up an apple, he bit into it. Chewing thoughtfully for a moment he nodded his head. "These will do fine." The man motioned the driver to pull forward. When the truck stopped, he reached inside for a cashbox and counted out $250 in fifty dollar bills.

With the help of four pickers, we loaded all the apples on the truck. As the driver covered them with a tarpaulin, Cecil reminded me, "I'll be back next Friday for fifty more bushels." The big truck drove away slowly, and with a smile, I walked back to the cider mill.

CHAPTER TWENTY-FIVE

A church group from Beloit showed up and bought fifty gallons for their fall picnic. A resort owner from Wautoma sent two men with a truck for seventy-five gallons. I had to make a trip to Merrill to buy 100 more empty jugs.

The weather was milder this fall with less humidity and a few overnight rain showers. The pickers worked steadily from dawn till five in the afternoon. After the last load of apples came in, they still had to be made into cider. I often didn't get back to the house until nine at night. Ardyce always had something for me to eat. Reuben was asleep when I left in the morning and was asleep when I got home. Sam, the dog, slept next to his cradle. This year I couldn't wait for the harvest to be over so I could spend more time with my family.

Cecil Andrews arrived every Friday afternoon for his fifty bushels of apples. John Pickett returned all the empty jugs from Lake Geneva and bought one-hundred more jugs of cider. As the season wore on, more local folks came to get one or two jugs.

"It just ain't fall without some cider," was the standard answer. Jake had offered the Jenske brothers the strainer barrels for one dollar a barrel. They agreed if they got a free jug of cider— another deal that would pay dividends at smoked ham time.

The ore company from Superior sent two men with a truck and bought fifty gallons. Never having tasted cider, I put the cup under the spigot, drew about a half cup and handed it to them. After taking a sip, one of the men licked his lips and said, "you better load another ten gallons."

Something was bound to go wrong, and the REO truck was to blame. It came in from the field coughing and misfiring, barely making it to the door where it died. We unloaded the apples, and with a little help from Elmer and Luther pushed it to the side of the barn.

I immediately called Billy Dehn at the garage who said, "It sounds like a clogged fuel line. When I close at five, I'll come out and fix it." Billy was right. He got under the hood, took out a thin metal pipe, blew through it, put it back on, worked the choke and it started right up running smooth.

"We will never be able to eat all this corn, Aaron. Let's give some to the workers," Ardyce suggested.

Jake and I loaded a bushel basket with ears of corn and carried it to the campsite, making sure every family received some. I wondered what Ardyce would give away next, probably tomatoes or carrots. It went to people who needed it, and we were glad to share.

I was at the gas station in Merrill getting three five-gallon gas cans filled for the REO. I followed the attendant inside to pay when I heard the gunfire. The bank was a half-block up the street from where I was. I stepped outside and saw two men rush out of the bank door. Both were holding pistols, and one had a satchel.

As they ran toward a waiting Ford Model A, a police car with the siren blowing turned the corner and headed toward them. The driver of the Model A got out and started shooting at the police car with his pistol. The two robbers from the bank yelled at the driver to get back in the Ford. The police car stopped, and two officers got out, the driver with a pistol and the other with a shotgun! BOOM! BOOM! The officer with the shotgun fired twice, and the getaway driver flew backward against the Ford and slid to the ground.

The other two robbers dropped their guns and threw their hands in the air, hollering, "We give up! We give up!" The officers made them lie down and handcuffed them. Someone from the bank ran out and grabbed the satchel. He opened it and showed the police, then took it back into the bank. The gas station attendant and I stared at each other wide-eyed, realizing we had just witnessed a failed bank robbery. Still shaking from the excitement, I got in the pickup truck and drove home to the safety of the cider mill.

I heard later from Sheriff Hobart that no one in the bank had been hurt. The three robbers had held up a bank in Rhinelander but had gotten very little money, so they tried again in Merrill.

"These hard times are bringing the outlaws farther north, so you be watchful," was his warning. We now kept my .12 gauge shotgun loaded and ready in the cider mill, just in case. As another precaution I had the electric company install a yard light. I don't know if it stopped any human intruders, but it did provide some entertainment.

CHAPTER TWENTY-SIX

At around eleven o'clock at night, I was checking some paperwork before bed when Sam, the dog, began whining and barking at the door. I had just let him out and back in an hour before so knew it must be something else that got his attention.

Pushing Sam back, I opened the door and stepped out on the porch. Four raccoons were scratching at the entrance to the cider mill! There were two larger and two smaller raccoons, probably a family looking for food. Sensing someone was there, they scuttled off into the darkness.

It was September, and the orchard was only about half empty. Truckloads of full apple baskets just kept coming in. Even with the government food program taking fifty bushels every week, I feared a lot of apples would go to waste. The cider was moving well with about twenty-five or thirty left at the end of each day.

One morning, Ardyce came up with the idea that appealed to everybody. "Let's donate some apples to the school and the local churches. It will not only build some goodwill but will let people know we are still in business."

Ardyce and Lilly took charge, and on Wednesday morning, they loaded several bushels onto Jake's pickup truck and took off. They came back that afternoon with an empty truck and some good news.

"The schools thrilled to get the apples," she said. "But the churches couldn't see the advantages. I told them we also made cider, but they were still dubious until I mentioned that hard cider was another form of wine. All the churches are having problems obtaining wine for services because of prohibition. I let them know that hard cider makes itself if you let it ferment for two months. They thanked me for the apples and said they would be coming out for cider."

Two men were sitting under the oak tree in the yard one morning as I stepped out on the porch with my coffee. When they saw me, they got up and came forward. They were average height and build and looked in good shape.

One stuck out his hand and said, "I'm Hank, my friend is Tom, and we are looking for work."

"Can you handle an axe and a saw?" I asked.

"We sure can, what do you pay?"

"I need firewood," I told them. "You give me a day's work, and I'll pay a dollar each." I got them an axe and a saw from the barn and directed them to the woodlot. "Just cut it into lengths and I'll pick it up later."

At noon Jake took some sandwiches and a jug of water out to the woodlot. When he came back, he was smiling. "You might want to hold on to those two. They cut more in a morning than you, me and Elmer cut in a day." Hank and Tom walked back to the house at about five o'clock.

I handed each a silver dollar and said, "Jake says you two did a good day's work. Would you like to keep working for a week? You can sleep in the barn, and I'll bring you supper here on the porch.

Both men gave a big grin, Hank shook my hand and said, "Throw in a jug of that cider, and you got a deal."

All across America, men were on the move. They walked, hitchhiked, and when possible, rode the empty boxcar of a train. The newspapers dubbed them hobo's and the name stuck. The railroad owners employed men armed with clubs to check all boxcars before and after a trip. Hobos learned to wait until the train started moving before trying to hitch a free ride and to jump off before it came to a stop.

In certain areas close to train yards, they congregated in makeshift camps called hobo jungles. They shared food, information, and stories of close calls. It never occurred to the railroad tycoons that they were mostly responsible for the hobos. Their hand in the stock market crash put many of these men out of work. I guess you reap what you sow.

CHAPTER TWENTY-SEVEN

By the first of October, three-quarters of the orchard had been picked. By the end of the day, the shelves would be holding up to thirty jugs of cider.

"Don't fret," Jake said. "You got a big sale coming soon." As usual, Jake was right. On a Friday afternoon, a black Cadillac rolled in and parked. The driver got out, came around, and opened the back door. A heavyset man with grey hair wearing a blue pin-striped suit and shiny shoes stepped out and looked around. I met him halfway across the yard.

Holding out his hand, he said in a deep voice, "My name is Leon Winkelman. I own a large Department store in Wausau. I have been getting reports from my staff concerning the fine quality of your cider. I'm hosting a large gathering of my business associates on the twenty-first of this month. Since liquor is prohibited, I thought I would serve cider. Can you fill an order of one-hundred gallons?"

Sensing an opportunity, I replied, "I believe I can, sir, but it may involve working my employees overtime."

With a slight wave of his hand, he said, "If you can fill the order, I will pay one dollar per gallon and will pick it up on the nineteenth. Do we have a deal?"

"I do require cash payment on delivery. If that is acceptable then yes, we have a deal." Shaking my hand again, he retreated to his Cadillac and drove slowly away. Jake had been watching from the doorway. He just nodded his head.

I finally found some time on a Saturday afternoon to bring in some of the firewood that Hank and Tom had cut. I backed the REO up to the woodlot, and Elmer and I got out to load up. The wood was cut and stacked in neat rows. The brush was piled out of the way and layered neatly.

"Those two men must have done this before," Elmer said. "They sure did a fine job."

We spent the afternoon loading the truck, taking turns being on the truck or the ground. Some would go to the stack by the backdoor for cooking, but most would be split and tossed down an open cellar window to be used in the furnace this winter. It was a good mix of hard and softwood that would keep the house warm.

We all heard the sirens coming down Wolf Creek Road.

"That's the fire truck's siren," Jake said. Everything stopped dead still as we watched the fire truck go by. In the distance, we could see a thin column of gray smoke rising skyward.

"Looks like it's coming from Harvey Lundgren's farm," Jake said.

Mildred had just parked the REO by the doors, and we were getting ready to unload more apples.

"Elmer, keep things running. Jake and I will be back soon," I yelled over my shoulder as I ran to catch up with Jake.

We spun up a little gravel as we took off out of the yard in the pickup. Hearing another siren behind us, we pulled over to let the pumper truck go by.

"Harvey is our local blacksmith," Jake said. "I'll bet the forge got too hot again."

"Has this happened before?" I asked.

"Yep, about three years ago, but that time he and his son managed to put it out before it got too bad. Looks like it got away from him this time."

Jake parked on the road so as not to block the drive, and we walked in. The forge was a roofed over lean-to next to the machine shed. As we got close, we could feel the heat and see that the forge and the shed were on fire. Men were dragging haying equipment out into the yard. The pumper was hosing down the flames with little effect.

Men with buckets and wet burlap sacks were beating out the sparks in the grass and weeds to keep the fire from spreading. The machine shed was old, tinder-dry, and the fire burned it to the ground. Within an hour, the fire burned itself out, leaving a smoking pile of embers. Everything in the forge was a total loss.

The pumper truck ran until the tank went dry, watering down the glowing fire-pit. Without saying a word, Jake and I drove back to the cider mill.

Mr. Winkelman sent two men in a new Chevrolet stake-bed truck to pick up his order. We carefully packed the jugs in straw-filled boxes and stacked them inside. The driver tied them down and pulled the tarpaulin cover over the load. He then reached in the truck, got out a clipboard, and handed me an envelope.

"Mr. Winkelman wants you to count the money then sign for it," the driver instructed.

Inside were five twenty-dollar bills and a slip, which I signed and gave back to him. He tipped his hat, got in the truck, and drove away.

CHAPTER TWENTY-EIGHT

I could hear the pickers yelling as they followed the truck in from the orchard. "Last load, Last load!" Mildred honked the horn to let us know it was real.

The last week of October brought cooler nights, sometimes almost cold. Many hands helped unload the bushels of ripe apples. The man from the food program would pick up his apples tomorrow, so we set those aside. Three people were waiting to buy, four more bushels gone. The shelves were about half full of jugs waiting for buyers.

I told the pickers, "Before you leave, take all the apples you want." I would pay them tomorrow morning as they were packed and ready to move on.

Several of my regular workers had stayed on to help with the cleanup. Calvin and Eugene washed down the grinder and cleaned the press. Mildred and Lottie, along with Luther, were taking down the campsites and bringing in the water barrels. All the apples were gone finally, but I had one hundred fifty jugs of cider left to sell. As the day passed, customers showed up. By five o'clock I was down to one hundred jugs.

Ardyce came out on the porch and yelled, "Aaron, telephone for you!"

I picked up the receiver to hear the voice of Mr. Leon Winkelman. "Mr. Stroud, I wish to relay to you my compliments on your fine cider. It was a big hit with my fellow businessmen. I want to send them each a gallon for the upcoming holidays. How many do you have available?"

"I have one-hundred gallons left sir, how many would you like?"

"I will take them all at our usual price. A truck will pick them up tomorrow. It is a pleasure doing business with you. I hope we can continue to do so." I gave Ardyce a hug that left her breathless.

I went out and told Jake the good news. Pointing his pipe at me and smiling, Jake said, "Old Leon is going to let them jugs sit and ferment. His friends will have hard cider for Christmas."

We dedicated the next few weeks to cutting and hauling firewood for me, Jake and Elmer. Jake's woodlot was twice the size of mine with plenty of oak, ash and elm trees.

Somehow, I got the REO backed up on a sharp rock and blew out a tire. It took a half-day to jack up the truck, remove the tire and take it into Billy Dehn at the garage. Billy was because I tipped him a dollar for doing a rush job. By late afternoon, the tire was back on the truck. Later, I would spend many happy hours splitting the big pieces into stove wood.

We hooked the plow back on the REO truck just in time. That night, it snowed, dropping a foot of downy flakes across the north woods. Elmer had arrived just as the snow was ending. He plowed our drive and took off on his route. About an hour later, he came back. He parked by the barn and blew the horn. I put on my coat and went out to see what the problem was.

"I hit a deer with the plow!" Elmer was all smiles holding up the head of a four-point buck. "I came around the curve by Lundgren's farm, and he just jumped out in front of me. Let's hang him in the barn, and you can dress him out while I finish plowing."

"I'm thinking venison roast for Thanksgiving," I told him. Ardyce called Jake, and we had the deer skinned, and half cut up before Elmer returned. We took turns carrying meat into the house where Ardyce, Lilly, and June wrapped it in butcher paper and made three piles, one for each family. Sam, the dog, got his first taste of real meat and begged for more.

Ardyce canned some of the venison and made another stew for supper. The aroma filled the house. Later, I dozed off by the fireplace holding my son.

In bed, later that night, I asked Ardyce if she ever missed living in Lansing. "I don't miss Lansing. This is our home, and I wouldn't change that for anything," was her reply.

CHAPTER TWENTY-NINE

We had the Thanksgiving feast at our home. Elmer and June arrived first with their daughter Louise. June was a happy lady. She and Elmer were expecting their second child. Jake and Lilly brought their daughter Francine, who Ardyce and I had not met yet. She had graduated from the Teacher College in Oshkosh and was teaching at the grade school in Tomahawk.

The big news was the auto and passenger train wreck in Kenosha. The driver of the car had tried to beat the train at the crossing and failed. Fifty-five people were dead and hundreds injured. Otherwise, the talk ran to the coming winter and the depression.

Little Reuben and Sam played on the rug in front of the fireplace. About one o'clock, Ardyce called, "Everyone to the table, the roast is ready."

What a meal! The venison roast, potatoes, gravy, carrots, green beans, cranberries, hot rolls and two kinds of pie—pumpkin and blackberry. I broke out the hard cider and toasted the day and the friends we shared it with.

I did the accounting books one afternoon. After wages and expenses, we had made $2,250 for the year. There was still the tax bill to settle, and Christmas was right around the corner, but despite the deplorable state of the economy the apple orchard gave Ardyce, Reuben, Sam and I a good living.

Ardyce decided we should do our Christmas shopping at Winkelman's Dept. Store in Wausau. She had been making a list since the middle of November and was pretty vocal about what she wanted.

"I need a new winter coat and an electric iron," she stated firmly. I would get some new flannel shirts, wool socks, and work gloves. Leaving Reuben and Sam in Lilly's care, we drove into Wausau.

It was an experience! We had never seen so many things in one place — four stories of anything you could ever want. Ardyce picked out several types of fabric to make into curtains, aprons, table cloths and outfits for Reuben and probably June's expected baby. A table of mismatched towels at five cents each got her attention. She got her new coat plus a shirt and blouse. The iron was next along with a waffle maker. The basket I was carrying was full, so Ardyce got another. My shirts, socks, and gloves came next. Then we moved to the children's section.

Her eyes lit up like stars as she picked out a new blanket, two warm outfits, toys, and baby oil. Then we needed wrapping paper and ribbon. Some Christmas candy and ornaments for the tree completed the list.

Finally, Ardyce wound down like an old clock and said, "I think that's enough." The total cost was $41.50, actually less than I expected. The panel van was packed full on the way home. We unloaded everything in the spare room then went to pick up Reuben and Sam. A busy day ended with leftover rabbit stew and homemade bread. Life was good.

Christmas morning dawned bright with the temperature at 25 degrees. Lounging by the fire with a cup of coffee, I watched Ardyce trying a new outfit on Reuben. Suddenly, Sam started barking and ran to look out the window. Thinking maybe a deer had wandered into the yard, I got up to look.

A big black bear was standing on his hind legs pounding on the cider mill door! He must have smelled the residue of the cider run. I got my shotgun, poked in two shells, and stepped out on the porch. I fired into the air. BANG! BANG! The bear fell backward in his haste to get away. Rolling in the snow for a few seconds before he finally got his feet under him and took off through the empty campsite. I lost sight of him as he went over a small hill headed for the creek. He had looked well-fed, so maybe he just wanted one more meal before he crawled into his den.

Jake had parted with one of his chickens for our Christmas dinner. Afterward, we carried more presents to the van, dressed Reuben, wrapped him in a blanket and drove to Jake and Lilly's. Elmer and June were there when we arrived.

Ardyce had been busy on her sewing machine. She made two aprons each for June, Lilly and Francine and a small one for Louise. Elmer and Jake got lined leather gloves for the cold weather. Ardyce and I got matching wool sweaters. Francine came out of the pantry carrying a tray with a half-bottle of plum brandy and seven small glasses.

"This is Dad's secret hoard of liquor," she told us. "Let's have a toast to the day and to family and friends."

Later that evening, Ardyce and I sat on the sofa holding Reuben between us. Sam was stretched out on the rug by the fireplace. We talked husband and wife talk: the baby, the bills, the house, and the Teeters family. It seemed like years had passed since we left Lansing on our honeymoon journey. I said a silent 'Thank you' to Dad, wishing he were here to see his dream come to life.

CHAPTER THIRTY

It was a week after New Year's day 1931. Light powder snow had fallen overnight, and the temperature hovered at ten degrees above zero. I had strung a clothesline in the spare bedroom. It looked like the back room of a Chinese laundry and smelled of soap and bleach. Reuben was nine months old, and the bulk of the wash was diapers.

The radio was tuned to a station in Milwaukee. The news was still all about the country sliding into a depression. One in four men were out of work nationwide. Factory workers were striking for fewer hours and more pay. Bank robberies were on the rise; soup kitchens were doing a booming business. Churches had taken to letting the homeless sleep in their basements at night during freezing weather. Those who had jobs saw their wages cut in half. What you paid a dollar for in 1929 cost a nickel today, and the Government had found no way to stop the collapse from happening.

"We are going to raise chickens," Ardyce informed me one afternoon. Thinking a minute, the idea appealed to me.

"I'll get Elmer to help me build a chicken coop attached to the side of the barn," I replied. It was a great idea. We would have fresh eggs every day and an occasional fried chicken dinner. I had thought about raising rabbits like Jake was doing, but had never followed through. The chickens *would* happen.

"Ardyce, I'm taking Sam for a walk," I said as I put on my boots, coat, and cap. I loaded some birdshot in the .12 gauge shotgun and followed Sam out the door. We walked down toward Wolf Creek, the snow, about a foot deep, packed underfoot. The temperature held steady at 25 degrees with a clear sky. Sam gave a short woof and stopped with one foreleg raised. I bought the gun up just as two grouse exploded from the tall grass. BANG! One grouse dropped, the other veered off to the left and out of sight. Sam retrieved the dead grouse, gently picked it up and carried it to me.

Kneeling, I stroked his head. "Good dog, Sam," I said softly. He was not yet a year old, and already, his instincts were coming out. Within an hour, we had bagged one more bird and then walked back to the house.

Ardyce stepped out on the porch to greet us. "Fresh grouse for supper," I said with a smile.

"You clean them, and I'll roast them," was the word from the boss.

The singer sewing machine was a constant sound in the house.

"What are you making now?" I asked my lovely wife.

Holding up a half-finished garment, she replied, "I'm making a dress for June's daughter Louise. If it turns out as it should, I'll try one for me."

She had purchased several yards of cloth on our trip to Wausau along with some dress patterns. There were new curtains throughout the house, although the cellar windows had somehow escaped her attention. On Saturday afternoons, Lilly and June visited to help with a patchwork quilt for the bed. Two of my old flannel shirts had been donated to this cause along with one each of Jake and Elmer's. Reuben, Sam and I wisely kept out of the way, often curled up on the sofa with a good book. Reading softly to Reuben usually put him to sleep laying on my stomach while Sam snored stretched out by the fireplace. These were the afternoons I would treasure in my memory for years to come.

"You hold her head, I'll hold her tail," were the directions I got from Jake. One of his Holstein heifers was having a little trouble with her first calf. Taking off his shirt, Jake gently reached in to help turn the calf's head. With a mighty push and a long grunt, the new-born slid out into the bed of hay we had laid down.

"Got another heifer," Jake informed me. We got the calf standing on its wobbly legs and let the new mother sniff and lick her baby. Jake guided the calf to the udder, and we watched as it took its first feeding, butting its head when the milk wasn't coming fast enough. This would give Jake another milker for his small herd. Although the price of milk was way down, it still paid enough to make a living. Farmers were hard-pressed during the depression, and many simply gave up and sold out. Jake and Lilly had their farm paid off, which helped keep them ahead of the hard times yet to come.

CHAPTER THIRTY-ONE

On February 5, 1931, Wilbur Stokley, Bryce Nieman, and Charlie Bennett, all in their twenties, began their short life of crime by robbing a bank in Superior. Their goal was to make a name for themselves by robbing banks all the way to Chicago.

Turning left out of Superior, their next stop was Ashland. The bank there was small and yielded less than $500. Wilbur fancied himself the leader and to show his friends he was not to be trifled with, he shot the bank manager in the leg. Woodruff was the next town of any size, but the only place open was a Savings & Loan. Again their haul was meager — about $200, taking all the coins.

Stopping for gas on the way out of town, they robbed the gas station and severely beat the owner. By the time they drove into Tomahawk, they felt invincible. They parked in front of the bank, got out, left the motor running, and entered the bank. Any luck deserted them at this moment as two local boys wandered by and thought it would be great fun to drive the car a block and park it, then watch the owner look for it.

Inside the bank, Charlie Bennett fired a shot into the ceiling to get everyone's attention. Wilbur ordered all the money put into a bank bag and given to him. Bryce had all the patrons lie down on the floor. The assistant manager pushed the silent alarm button without being noticed. It took a few minutes to gather all the money. A teller had trouble closing the bank bag, as it was so full. Wilbur was laughing at this, thinking this big score would take them to Chicago.

The three robbers backed out of the bank, then turned around to find their car gone! They ran into the street, hoping to steal a car. The first car they saw was a police car followed by two other police cars. Whether in anger or panic, Wilbur fired on the first police car. The car stopped, and the two officers inside came out shooting. Wilbur was shot twice in the body and once in the throat and died where he fell. Bryce and Charlie tried to run for it, shooting as they ran. A shotgun blast broke Charlie's left leg. He toppled over, dropped his gun, grabbed his leg, and screamed, "I give up!"

Bryce was the only one not shot because he threw himself down on the street, tossed his gun in the gutter, and yelled, "Please, don't shoot me!"

Wilbur's body went unclaimed, and they buried him in a County cemetery with only his name and date of death on the small tombstone. Bryce and Charlie were both given twenty years in the state prison in Green Bay. Charlie's leg never healed properly, and he limped the rest of his life. Bryce served five years then was killed by another prisoner for reasons unknown. The two boys who had moved the car later told the police what they had done. They were not charged with stealing a car but were told never to do it again.

Fortunately, Jake and Elmer knew how to build a chicken house. We got the chicken wire from the hardware store along with nails and hinges. The lumber and the door came next from the sawmill. All this was loaded on Jake's pickup truck and hauled home. We unloaded everything in the barn and set to work. The coop would be a lean-to structure with the entry from the barn. An opening was cut for the door, framed in and hinged up. We laid down a wood floor and framed the sides and roof.

A small hinged entrance for the chickens that could be secured at night had a slight ramp that led out to the back of the barn. The large area was fenced in with wire to give the chickens a place to walk and feed on whatever they could find. This would put them out of the way during the apple harvest.

Ardyce had decided she wanted a dozen hens and a rooster. Jake would supply these when the hens he had setting hatched their eggs. We agreed on 50 cents a chick. A couple of bales of straw for nests and two bags of chicken feed were waiting in the barn.

My wife was now a chicken farmer and couldn't wait to get started.

Sam and I did another grouse hunt. I just let him range out in front of me with his nose to the ground. He would never win a field trial for pointing, but he always found birds. When he got their scent, he slowed down, stopped, and then gave a woof! It was enough to put the grouse in the air, and then it was up to me. Two more birds made it to the oven at home. Good boy Sam!

CHAPTER THIRTY-TWO

Spring in Wisconsin is a stop and start ritual that is frustrating and filled with hope at the same time. Two warm and sunny days will be followed by rain and cold and an occasional ice storm. The sun will make another encore followed by snow, followed by rain and then a few more days of warm sunny weather. Eventually, the sun will win the day, and winds from the southwest will dry the land. The flowers will push their way through the soil to bring color to a brown landscape. The first green grass is the promise fulfilled, and the buds on the trees are the final sign of the warm weather to come.

Looking out the front window one morning, I saw a familiar sight. Sitting under the oak tree in the yard were Hank and Tom! They had done a great job cutting firewood last year, and now they were back.

"Ardyce, we need two cups of coffee and a couple of cinnamon rolls." I stepped out on the porch and motioned for the men to come up and sit.

"We were hoping you might have some work for us," Hank said.

Ardyce bought out a tray with the coffee and rolls, saying, "Before you talk work, have some breakfast."

I asked them how they made it through the winter.

"We worked in a logging camp up on the Brule River," Tom said between sips of coffee. "The mills in Wausau are still in business and still need lumber, but the log drive is over."

I decided on a long-range work plan for these two hard workers. "If I find work for you this summer, will you stay around for the apple harvest?"

They looked at each other, then at me, and Hank replied, "We were hoping we could work all summer. Whatever you need done, we can do it."

"I sure would like to find out how you make that cider," Tom said with a smile.

Thinking a minute, I offered, "I'll make a trip to Merrill and get some lumber. Your first job will be to build two bunk beds in the barn — no more sleeping on the floor. Also, you will take supper with us in the house. I'll pay you each five dollars a week."

We shook hands on the deal and went to clear a space in the barn.

Ardyce sewed two long bags of heavy flannel that would be stuffed with straw for mattresses. She also went through my older clothing, saying, "They will need a change of clothing so I can wash theirs. Take the washtub out to the barn and heat some water. If they are going to eat in the house, they will be clean and presentable."

When they were told what was expected both laughed. "Your wife is absolutely right, bring on the hot water!"

Jake and Elmer agreed to share the cost when Hank and Tom worked for them. There was first crop hay to put up, corn to plant and more wood to cut. Four more hands would make life a little easier for all of us.

Wisconsin received a little federal money to help during the depression. Several crews were put to work rebuilding roads and bridges. Keeping idle hands busy was a way to cut down the petty crime that had sprung up.

Numerous minor break-ins had occurred around Merrill. Farmers had chickens go missing; store owners reported windows broken on storerooms and stock pilfered. Hungry men without jobs will resort to thievery to survive. Sheriff Hobart and two deputies were kept busy day and night.

In March of 1931, Congress passed the Davis-Bacon act requiring contractors and sub-contractors to pay the prevailing wages to all employees for all federal work projects over $2,000. Contractors fought this law for several reasons. This meant paying Mexicans and Negroes the same wages as whites. It also meant bidding on work in an area where sometimes wages were higher than expected.

Federal inspectors were sent out to make sure contractors were complying with the law. Several inspectors were threatened, and one in Texas was severely beaten. Federal Marshals were pressed into service to protect the inspectors. After a few contractors were arrested and charged, things settled down.

Congress promised to amend the law to make it more friendly. Whether this law would help or hurt the economy was yet to be determined. It did, however, put men back to work.

CHAPTER THIRTY-THREE

Ardyce was in a house cleaning frenzy. It was April. Every window in the house was open, the curtains washed and left drying on the line. Hank and Tom were washing windows, and I was mopping floors. Reuben was a year old and walking. He and Sam were wrestling under the dining room table. I had cleaned the fireplace out the day before and spread the ashes on the garden plot.

"I need some more hot water," Ardyce yelled from the bathroom. She was washing out the bathtub and scrubbing the sink. "Don't forget to beat the rug."

The living room rug was hanging from a lower branch of the oak tree waiting to have the dust beaten out. The spring routine in Wisconsin was repeated down Wolf Creek Road, across Lincoln County, and throughout the State.

The grass was growing, the flowers were blooming, and the apple trees were a riot of color. Bees and hummingbirds filled the air as they pollinated the blossoms. Hank and Tom were picking up the fallen branches. They would be bundled and given to the Jenske brothers to smoke their hams later.

"It looks like this branch was broken off," Tom called.

He was right. "That damn bear is going to have to be found and shot," I said.

"I think I know where he had his winter den," Hank replied. "We probably should take care of him before the apples come out, or he'll be breaking more branches."

I had hoped the bear would move on, but he decided he liked apples. It was time to get rid of this menace before any more damage was done.

Elmer, Hank and I loaded up and headed down to the creek. I had my 30.06 Springfield, Hank got the .12 gauge shotgun with slugs, and Elmer had his Winchester 30.30.

Jake decided to sit this hunt out. "I'm getting too old to be chasing bears that ain't chasing me."

The day was warm, with a breeze from the west. We found fresh tracks in the mud along Wolf Creek. Elmer took the lead and moved slowly ahead. Hank followed second, with Tom next carrying the rope. I covered our back. The wind shifted from the northwest bringing with it the rank odor of the bear. Elmer stopped, looked around, and then looked up. Scanning the treeline, I thought I saw movement in an elm tree to our left.

"I think the bear might be in that big elm," I whispered.

As we moved closer, the bear shifted its weight to move around to the other side of the tree. Moving slowly, we circled the elm until I got a good view.

BANG! BANG! BOOM!

We all three fired at once! The bear jerked, rolled sideways and toppled out of the tree. He was dead when he hit the ground.

The bear had wintered well. He was lean, but the fur was in excellent shape. We tied the rope around the front quarters and took turns dragging the carcass back home.

We hung the bear in the oak tree and skinned it out. I was set on having the hide tanned for a living room rug. Fortunately, Ardyce liked the idea. Judging by the teeth, this was an older bear, and the meat would be tough and stringy when cooked.

"There's a big hole where a tree blew down a few years ago in Dad's woodlot. Let's bury it there" Elmer offered. Jake had no objections, so into the hole it went. The hide went into Merrill where it would take months to turn it into a rug.

The first crop hay always brings the smell of summer. Jake was driving his Case tractor with the wagon behind, towing the hayloader. Elmer and I caught the grass as it hit the wagon and spread it around to get an even load. When the cart was full, Jake drove to the barn and pulled up under the haymow. An overhead beam jutted out, holding a big four-prong lift on a pulley. The prongs were stomped into the hay, allowing them to grab a huge load of hay that was lifted into the air. The hay was then pulled into the mow by Hank and Tom who pulled the release rope dropping the grass down to be spread around. The big prongs were pulled back up and sent back out for another load.

With some luck, there would be two more crops of hay to fill the mow to overflowing. This would take Jake's herd through the winter. After Jake's first hay crop was in, we would move to Elmer's and repeat the process.

With the depression, farming hardly paid. The price of milk was so low some farmers were threatening to go on strike and dump their milk rather than sell it.

"Seems kinda dumb to me, it would make more sense to give it to the needy," was Jake's opinion.

Ardyce and I walked the apple orchard one evening. I carried Reuben on my shoulders, and Sam was following. Reuben would reach up to grab the leaves on the trees as we passed under them. After he smelled the leaves, he dropped them in my hair.

He was filling out his small body, and I could tell he would be built like my Dad. His dark curly hair was soft as silk. His blue eyes sparkled when he laughed, which was often. Sam was his best friend, playmate, and bodyguard. He kept Reuben out of everything except mud puddles, in which they played in together, much to my wife's dismay. While she bathed Reuben, I washed down Sam. A father's work is never done.

CHAPTER THIRTY-FOUR

The chickens had settled into their new home. Ardyce cared for them like a mother hen, making sure they had food and water. We loved having fresh eggs every morning, occasionally Hank and Tom would join us.

The rooster liked Ardyce, tolerated me, and was not happy with Sam. He would fly at the wire fence whenever Sam walked by. Sam thought it was another game, and would 'woof' softly to see the rooster do it again.

The garden was in and growing. Tom seemed to have a green thumb, weeding and watering the vegetables as they pushed their way up through the soil. Hank was the handyman, always checking for loose boards or a hinge that needed mending.

They both were a big help cleaning out the fireplace and pulling a small pine up and down the chimney to clean out the soot build-up. Unless this was done, the soot could re-ignite when the first fire of the winter was started. The burning soot would be carried up to land on the roof where the dry cedar shakes would burn like tinder.

Lilly was teaching Ardyce to knit. It was slow going at first as she learned how to inter-weave the yarn into something that resembled an actual pattern. Her first wool scarf did not meet her exact standards and was pulled apart and redone. Her second attempt was much better, and she moved on to knitting a cap for Reuben. We would sit in the living room in the evening with Reuben and Sam wrestling on the rug. I would read the Herald newspaper, and Ardyce patiently rocked in her chair, hum a song and gently work the big needles, making another scarf or cap. The radio often played in the background, another world, far away.

On a Friday night in early June 1931 two brothers, Sidney Marshall, age 23 and Calvin Marshall, age 25 entered a 'gentlemen's club' on Main street in Hurley. They paid two dollars each to enter a backroom where they served beer and liquor. Keeping to themselves at the end of the bar, they listened to a jazz band while watching couples dance.

One couple seemed to be arguing. The woman slapped the man, who then slapped the woman. She reached into her beaded purse, took out a small handgun, and shot the man in the chest twice. Still holding the gun, she turned to run out the backdoor and ran right into Calvin Marshall.

In a panic, she shot Calvin, hitting him in the upper arm. The first man the woman shot was Frank Sylvester. His friend Benny 'Beaner' Cholo knelt by his side. Both were members of the Joe Saltis gang. Benny pulled a double-action colt from a shoulder holster and shot the woman in the back, killing her instantly.

The bullet passed through her, hitting Sidney Marshall in the hip. The bartender grabbed a .12 gauge sawed-off double-barreled shotgun from under the bar and shot Benny.

Customers started yelling and screaming as they ran from the club. Frank Sylvester, not yet dead, grabbed Benny's gun and shot the bartender. When the police finally arrived on the scene, they found four people dead and two injured. The woman was later identified as Ada Barker. Sidney and Calvin Marshall were treated at the local hospital, then released pending a trial which never happened.

The 'gentlemen's club' was owned by Joe Saltis. It was closed for a year, sold to the brother of Al Capone, and reopened under a new name.

Judging by the number of apples on the trees, it was going to be a bumper crop year. The bear was gone, so the trees were safe. The problem now was raccoons. They didn't break any branches; they just ate apples until they were full, then came back night after night for more.

"I'll give Vernon Jackson a call; he'll trap out the raccoons. Everybody calls him 'Cooney' because his favorite thing is trapping coons," Elmer said.

This sounded like just what I needed. "Does he charge much?"

Chuckling, Elmer said, "He makes enough from selling the hides that he never charges. Give him a few jugs of cider in the fall, and he'll be a happy trapper."

In all, Cooney trapped out eight raccoons. "I think I got the whole family," he told me. "But if you have any more trouble, just let me know, and I'll be back."

Out of curiosity, I asked, "How much do you get for the hides?"

With a little smile, he told me, "The price of hides used to be good. I could get $15 for a big coon hide. Now I get 50 cents apiece. It ain't much, but I also trap muskrat, beavers, and mink which makes up for the coons."

Billy Dehn showed up to give the REO a checkup. He drained the radiator, checked for leaks and filled it back up. An oil change was needed after plowing all winter. He checked the fuel lines and tinkered with the carburetor. All the tires were checked and aired up.

Wiping his hands on a rag, he said, "I just love working on this old truck. I almost feel bad charging you $15, and that includes the oil."

"How is business in town?" I asked.

Pushing his cap back on his head with his thumb, he said, "I get by. I take care of the police and sheriff's cars plus the ambulance and most of the bigwigs' vehicles at the courthouse. It ain't what it used to be, but it's what I do."

He loaded his toolbox in his pickup truck and drove away. What he said seemed to be the attitude of America. Important people playing with money they didn't have had taken the country down to a bare existence. Now, we just kept doing what we have always done, but for a lot less money and even less trust in those at the top. Shakespeare was right when he said, 'The evil that men do lives after them.'

When I got back to the house, Ardyce was on the telephone with her father. I could tell by her actions this was not going to be good news.

She hung up the receiver and said, "Mom is in the hospital. Dad said she was having chest pains, so he took her to the doctor, and he checked her right in. He says it's her heart."

The tears were forming in her eyes as I held her close. Kissing her forehead, I said softly, "Pack a bag for you and one for Reuben. I'll call the train station and get a schedule for the trip to Lansing."

CHAPTER THIRTY-FIVE

Ardyce left the next afternoon. Reuben was having great fun waving at everyone. I kissed them both goodbye, knowing I would be missing them terribly by tonight. Sam would take it just as hard. He and Reuben had not been apart since he first arrived in a box as a puppy, a present from Luther.

Ardyce promised to call with the latest news when she arrived in Lansing. This would be the second time she visited her parents without me. The next time we would all go together. I wanted to visit my father's grave and thank him for the wonderful life he had given us.

Lilly brought over a casserole and June brought a chocolate cake. I told them I would keep them up-to-date on any news. Sam roamed the house all night looking for Reuben.

As Hank, Tom and Elmer helped me get the campsite ready, the white cottony clouds took on a gray fringe that slowly darkened. The wind picked up, and I could feel the promise of much-needed rain.

It began to drizzle that evening and turned into a steady rain that lasted most of the night. By morning the sun was out, and the air felt warm and clean — perfect corn-growing weather.

Sam was my constant shadow as I took inventory of jugs and corks in the cider house. Some of the baskets were beyond repair. I made a note to pick up replacements on my next trip to Merrill.

I picked up the receiver on the first ring of the telephone. It was Ardyce.

"Mom is doing better," she said. "The doctor put her on a diet to lose some weight. She had a mild stroke but should be fine."

"When are you and Reuben coming home?" I asked anxiously.

With a little laugh, she said, "We'll take the train out tomorrow morning. Reuben has been asking about you and Sam."

"Tell him Sam and I miss both of you, so hurry home."

I took Sam along to the train station. We waited patiently on the platform for the train to come to a stop. Ardyce was the fourth passenger to step down, holding Reuben. There was no stopping Sam when he saw them. With an excited bark, he ran toward them his tail spinning around wildly. Reuben was laughing and squirming around to be put down, and Ardyce obliged. The boy and the dog merged into one wriggling pile as they reunited. Holding my wife close, I hugged her until she gasped for breath and laughed.

"It's just so good to be home," she whispered in my ear.

"How are things in Lansing?" I asked on the drive home.

With a sigh, Ardyce explained, "The depression has turned the city upside down. Everyone is out of work, the soup and breadlines stretch for blocks, factories are closed, and it looks like there's no end in sight."

"Is your mom going to be alright?"

"As long as she sticks to her diet and loses some weight, the doctor said she would be out of danger."

Eunice had always been on the plump side, but age and worry can take its toll on everyone, even those in the best of health.

Patting her arm, I assured her, "Your father will see to it that the doctor's orders are followed."

For the next week, Reuben and Sam hardly let each other out of sight, making sure each knew where the other was. Sam was alert to any noise he deemed unusual. He even seemed to know each vehicle by sound as they drove into the yard. When Sheriff Hobart drove in, Sam gave a light growl, and his hackles rose on his neck.

I let the sheriff come to the door and invited him in. As Sam stood waiting for a sign, I greeted the sheriff warmly, shook his hand and invited him to sit. Sam relaxed and walked forward to be petted. When the sheriff pat Sam's head, scratched his ears and called him by name, the dog became the gentle good-natured dog he usually was. He was a hunter, guard dog, and family pet.

CHAPTER THIRTY-SIX

During the past winter, when the temperature hovered at five degrees below zero, and the furnace ran steadily, I had decided to do some research about apples. I had wondered why Dieter Grundvall had chosen the varieties of apple trees he had planted. Why those particular varieties of apples?

I started with the Granny Smiths. It intrigued me that this variety had originated in Australia in the 1860s. Its sweet taste and low acidity make it a prime apple for cider.

The Golden Delicious began its growth in Iowa in the 1890s. The mild flavor, sweet taste, and resistance to most diseases made it a good choice for a cider apple.

The Somerset originated in England in the early 1800s. It ripens early, has a long tree life and with its sweet, juicy flavor has long been a popular cider apple in England.

The McIntosh apple came from Canada. Dieter must have chosen this variety as the blender for all the others. It's tart flavor, higher acidity and early ripening time made it the perfect apple to bring out the taste and aroma of great cider.

Any one of these varieties also make a tasty pie or are perfect for eating right off the tree. Dieter had done his homework and chosen the best apples to make the best cider.

I decided on a few changes for the cider-making crew this year. I wanted Hank and Tom more involved in the process. This meant using a bit of diplomacy with Jake. About a week before the harvest began, I asked Jake, "How would it sit with you to be the overseer from now on? I need someone I can trust to take care of the problems that crop up every day, not just in the orchard but here at the mill."

Hooking his thumbs in the bib of his overalls, Jake thought a minute and then replied, "If you put Hank working the strainer and Tom carrying the buckets of apples to the grinder, I believe it could work out pretty good."

It gave me a little shiver up my back because that was the plan I had in mind! This older man seemed to be able to read my mind, but I would never let him know it.

"Why Hank on the strainer?" I asked.

"It takes somebody with an eye for detail, and that's Hank," he said. "Tom is more into a routine job, like carrying the buckets."

The first regular workers began arriving a few days later. The campground was ready, and the barrels filled with water. Mildred, the truck driver who lived in Merrill, came out to go over the REO. Calvin and Eugene Potts did some adjusting to the press. Hank and Tom were watching all this with anticipation, curious as to how the whole operation worked. I had told them about their jobs, and they were ready to make cider.

Jake had been very particular in training Hank on the strainer. "Don't work the paddle too hard; keep a steady motion. You will know when it needs cleaning," the old master said.

Most of my regular apple harvesters had returned, along with a half-dozen newcomers. I posted a sign by the road saying 'NO LONGER HIRING' to let the late arrivals know all the jobs were filled.

On the first morning, they all gathered by the big open doors of the cider mill. I explained the rules, let them all know what the pay was and then, after welcoming the new folks, I turned to Luther.

"Tell them what we are going to do," I said with a smile.

Luther hollered, "LET'S MAKE CIDER!"

The pickers followed the truck out to the orchard. Empty baskets stacked on the flatbed waited for another year's harvest.

Ardyce, Reuben, and Sam came out to gather eggs. When Sam saw Luther, his tail went into full wag, he gave a happy bark and ran right to him. Laughing, Luther gently held his head, rubbed his ears, and kissed his nose.

"Me too, me too," cried Reuben. Luther picked him up and hugged him. Reuben laughed and pinched Luther's nose!

Hugging me, Ardyce said, "We're going over to see June and Lilly later today, can you get by without us for a few hours?"

"I will be almost, but not quite, too busy to miss you," I said.

"Tell June I'll bring home some apples for pie," Elmer said.

We used ladders in the orchard to reach the top branches. Jake had Mildred carry a hammer and some nails on the truck just in case a rung let go. The windfalls that were too bruised to go in the grinder were tossed into a separate basket. They would go to the Jenske brothers along with the barrel from the strainer. For about two months, their pigs would eat high on the hog!

As the first truckload of apples came in, ready hands unloaded the baskets and gently dumped them into pails. Tom carried the buckets, two at a time, to the grinder and slowly poured them in. Elmer and Luther began turning them into the sauce that went into the press. Calvin and Eugene bore down on the auger, and the first cider ran down the trough to the cider pan. Lottie and her crew filled the jugs and corked them. It was all hard work, so I guess any cider made here was hard cider.

Having Jake as the overseer was already paying off. All the things that used to take up most of my day he now handled on the spot. A gouge from a tree branch got a bandage. A broken ladder rung was immediately fixed. A long bamboo pole was used to knock down apples too high to reach. A broken jug got swept up and thrown away. All this gave me time to deal with the customers that showed up for cider.

People trickled in two and three at a time. Sheriff Hobart made his stop, along with the District Attorney and a Judge. The price had gone from fifty cents to seventy-five cents a gallon, and no one seemed to mind.

CHAPTER THIRTY-SEVEN

Sunday morning, I was splitting some pine kindling for the cookstove when Ardyce walked up from the chicken house carrying a small basket of eggs and a frown on her pretty face.

Without waiting for me to ask, she said, "I'm missing a chicken."

"I'll look into it right after breakfast," I told her. I thought maybe one chicken had found a way under the fence and was out sightseeing. After breakfast, Sam and I went to inspect the fence wire. I had pegged the chicken wire down securely all around. It was still intact. As I was scratching my head, Sam got a sniff of something, gave a slight woof, and walked off. Thinking maybe a fox or a weasel, I followed.

With his nose to the ground, he headed for the campsite! I followed him as he circled the grounds to the farther corner where the newcomers were setup. Sam slowed, sniffed and stopped at the most distant campsite. A man, a woman and a boy about six- or seven-years-old sat by a cooking fire with a pot hanging over it.

"Good morning folks, what's for breakfast?" I asked.

"Just cooking some oatmeal," the woman mumbled.

"Mind if I have a look?"

"No need to look mister; it's just oatmeal," the man said as he stood. Sam gave a low growl, and his hackles rose on his back.

"Easy, Sam," I said.

"I came up missing a chicken this morning, and my dog led me here. I'm quite sure my chicken is in your cooking pot. If I'm wrong, then dish me up some oatmeal."

The woman was wringing her hands, and the boy had tears forming in his eyes. "Pack up your tent and be off my land in one hour," I told the man.

With a pleading look, the woman said, "We were hungry, and you have so much. We didn't think you would miss one chicken."

"If you needed food, you should have asked me. I would have given you enough for two meals. I won't have a thief on my land. I want to see that old Ford drive off my property in one hour. Let's go, Sam." I turned and walked away, and Sam followed.

Ardyce shook her head when I told her where her missing chicken went. I got a cup of coffee and waited out on the porch. I watched as their old Model T came down the track and drove slowly out of the yard. A few of my regular workers came to see what had happened. I explained the problem, and they all agreed it was the only thing to do.

"Next he would have been stealing from us," one of the women said. As they walked away, I knew they were right. A thief will not stop because his stomach is full. To that person, everything and everyone is fair game.

The next day, I explained to Jake what had happened.

"No big loss," he said. "That guy wasn't much of a worker anyway."

"I'm still trying to figure out just how he got the chicken."

"No big mystery there," Jake told me. "The man lifted his son over the fence, the boy went up the ramp, opened the small door, crawled in, and got a chicken. He then handed the chicken to his dad and was lifted back over the fence."

Of course! When I thought about it, it was the only way it could have happened.

"He was teaching his son to steal," I said.

Pointing his pipe at me, Jake said, "No matter how tough times are, stealing is never the answer."

CHAPTER THIRTY-EIGHT

At 9:15 a.m. on the twentieth of October, 1931, a 1928 Lincoln slowly came to a stop at the Kraft State Bank in Menomonie, Wisconsin. Frank Webber, Charlie Harmon, Frank Keating, and Tommy Holden got out of the car, looked around and walked into the bank. When Harmon hollered "This is a hold-up," the owner of the bank, William Kraft, pulled a short-barreled .38 Smith & Wesson pistol and shot and wounded Harmon.

Charlie Harmon returned fire, wounding Bill Kraft. Frank Keating ordered everyone except James Kraft, Williams' son, to lay down on the floor. Harmon held a gun to James' head while Keating and Tommy Holden emptied the vault and cashiers stations of $90,000.

Meanwhile, the guard, Vernon Townsend, somehow tripped the alarm. The robbers fled taking James Kraft and a cashier, Arlene Schafer, as hostages. Running to their Lincoln, Mrs. Schafer tripped and fell spraining her ankle. The robbers left her behind taking only James Kraft. As the car sped away, it came under fire from townspeople who had heard the alarm.

Winfeld Kern, Ed Grudt, and Vernon Townsend fired on the fleeing car as the robbers fired back. Ed Grudt was superficially wounded, and Frank Webber was killed—his lifeless body thrown from the vehicle by Tommy Holden.

The big Lincoln sped down Route 12 pursued by the sheriff and a deputy in a Ford Model A. To slow down the sheriff they shot and killed James Kraft and threw his body out onto the highway.

Charlie Harmon, who had been shot in the bank, died in the speeding car. Keating and Holden stopped, laid Harmon's body by the side of the road and made their getaway. For eight months they were the objects of a four-state search.

Acting on a tip from a young golf caddy, Frank Keating and Tommy Holden were surrounded and arrested on a Kansas City, Missouri golf course. They were tried and convicted in federal court and sentenced to life in prison at Leavenworth Penitentiary. The money was never recovered.

Cecil Andrews from the Government food program had renewed his request for fifty bushels of apples per week. As the initial panic of the depression settled down, people adjusted to the new low-key way of life and the demand for cider improved. A lot of the old regulars returned along with a few newcomers.

Hank and Tom handled their new jobs well. Things ran smoothly, and the cider flowed. By the end of each day, there were at most twenty or twenty-five jugs waiting to be purchased. Any problems that arose were taken care of by either Mildred or Jake.

Ardyce brought Reuben and Sam to the mill at the end of each day. Their day would not be complete without saying goodbye to Luther and Elmer.

Over supper, I asked Hank and Tom, "What plans do you guys have for this winter?"

Sipping his iced tea, Hank said, "We have a standing offer from the Oglethorpe Lumber Company. They are still cutting timber up on the Brule River. It's good money, good food, and a good crew to work with."

"I sure hope you both plan to come back here in the spring," Ardyce said.

With a big smile, Tom replied, "About the first of May start checking under your oak tree in the yard. As soon as we get the logs down-river, we'll be back."

The word must have spread among the resort owners about our cider. We got requests from a resort on Silver Lake in Wautoma and one from Fremont. They both said they would send a truck to pick up as many gallons as we could supply.

Mr. Winkelman from Wausau sent a letter stating his fondness for our cider and asked for one hundred gallons by the end of October. More hard cider for his friends at Christmas, I supposed.

The natural fermentation process is a miracle of nature. The very fine particles of apple in the pressed juice that make it look cloudy are called soft cider. Letting it sit at room temperature out of the light allows the pulp to release its natural sugar and yeast. Some foam will gather at the top as the process is underway. When the foam disappears, the hard cider is almost ready. To boost the alcoholic content, let the cider age like you would a fine wine. In about two months, the process is complete and ready to drink!

The cider barrels had never been used since Ardyce and I began making the cider. I had often wondered if Dieter had used them. I asked Jake if he had ever seen the barrels filled with cider.

"Old Dieter never got to fill them barrels," he said. "The cider sold so fast that the jugs were all he used."

"This year, let's fill one and see if we can sell it."

"I guess we could use a bucket and a funnel to fill it, but who would buy it?" Jake wondered.

"I'll bet Mr. Winkelman would be interested," I said.

Rubbing his chin with his thumb, Jake thought a minute and then replied, "By golly, you just might be right about that. He wants a hundred gallons in October. Two fifty-gallon barrels ought to fill the bill."

CHAPTER THIRTY-NINE

"Don't forget I need flour and two cakes of dry yeast," Ardyce hollered as I headed out the front door.

Ardyce, Lilly, and June had decided to bake loaves of bread for the pickers. "It's mostly for the children," Ardyce explained. "They need to eat more healthy foods."

I was going into Merrill for chicken feed, fifty more jugs, and gas for the REO truck. I hadn't been in town for more than a month. As I drove down Main, the dark display windows of closed businesses were a sad reminder that the depression still held its grip on Wisconsin.

A few hardy enterprising shop owners had survived by trading for goods. What had once been a clothing store was now a second-hand store. In the window was a gallon Red Wing jug. Out of curiosity, I stopped and went inside. The lady behind the counter smiled and asked, "What can I help you with today?"

"Do you have any more of the gallon jugs in the window?" I asked.

"I have two dozen of those Red Wings I can't sell. If you want them, I'll take two dollars for the whole bunch." I handed over two silver dollars. Loading the two boxes into in the panel truck, I went to get the flour and yeast.

Ardyce took one look at the red Wing jugs, and her brilliant mind took over.

"June is an amateur painter. I can have her paint the name of our cider mill on each jug."

Scratching my head, I reminded her, "Our cider mill doesn't have a name."

"Of course it does, Aaron. We live on Wolf Creek Road; the Wolf Creek runs through our property, so we are 'Wolf Creek Cider'!"

It made perfect sense. "I want the name painted on the mill, above the door, so everyone can see it," I told Ardyce.

With a smile, she said, "these jugs will be collector pieces. With the name painted on them, we will give them as gifts to Mr. Winkelman and the resort owners and even Mr. Cecil Andrews from the government food program."

That Saturday afternoon, I asked Hank and Tom if they wanted to make a little extra money. I explained how Ardyce and I wanted a sign above the door.

With his hands on his hips, Hank eyed the building and told Tom, "We need to measure how long the building is so we can center the letters. Then we measure the letter size and space them out, so they come out even. Using the first 'E' in CREEK as our center point, we work our way backward from the middle."

Turning to me, he continued, "We'll need two step ladders and some long planks to stand on. I'll also need a yardstick and some charcoal to draw letters. When we have it right, we paint in the letters. Sound good to you?"

"The ladders and planks are in the barn," I said. "And while you two are setting up, I'll find the yardstick and charcoal."

It took most of the afternoon and into the early evening to get the lettering just right. Hank seemed to have an artist's eye for this kind of work.

During supper, Hank said, "Tom and I would like to work on painting the letters tomorrow. There is a gallon of white paint in the barn that should show up real good."

"Have you done this kind of work before?" Ardyce asked.

"I used to paint houses in my younger days," Hank explained. "But this is my first time painting a sign. We will need some brushes and rags for cleanup."

Right after Sunday morning breakfast and coffee, Hank and Tom climbed their stepladders and began filling in the letters with white paint. Slowly and carefully, the sign took shape. This time they started at each end and worked toward the middle. Tom, having some painting experience, soon had WOLF filled in. A bit slower, Tom very carefully painted in CIDER. As they got to the center of the sign, Hank took over.

By noon CREEK was filled in. The men climbed down and stood back to look at their masterpiece. In bright white letters across the weathered wood of the mill, WOLF CREEK CIDER stood out for all to see.

Ardyce had called Jake and Lilly and soon their pickup truck rolled into the yard. "We should have done this a year ago," was Jake's reaction.

Jake and Lilly stayed for a lunch of egg-salad sandwiches and a garden salad with iced tea on the front porch. Several of the workers came from the campsite to see the new sign. All nodded their heads with approval.

After we finished eating, I handed Hank and Tom a five-dollar gold piece each. Their eyes got big, and their mouths dropped open.

"When you work for me on Sunday and do great work like that sign, you each earned every penny," I told them.

"I think I'll call the newspaper tomorrow and ask them to take a picture and run a story about this," Ardyce said, smiling.

Lilly clapped her hands. "That's a wonderful idea, and I bet it will sell some cider!"

Hank and Tom were almost blushing with pride. I thought back to the first day Ardyce and I had parked in the yard and viewed our new home. Outwardly, not much had changed. Overall, everything had changed. We had a home, a business, good friends, and a future.

CHAPTER FORTY

"That's a mighty pretty sign," Luther said with a big smile. Reuben was taking his morning ride on Luther's broad shoulders while Sam stood on his hind legs to get his ears scratched. "I'm gonna tell Dad to bring his girlfriend Lucy to see it."

Sheriff Hobart was a widower. His wife Alma had died during the Flu epidemic in 1919. Luther was 13 years old at the time and still talked about her. This was the first we had heard that Melvin Hobart had a lady friend.

Elmer stared upward at the sign and echoed his father's words saying, "We *should* have done that a year ago." As the customers arrived that day, almost every one of them remarked on the sign.

In her wisdom, Ardyce told me, "Now we need to have some labels printed up for the gallon jugs."

That afternoon, Dalton Fischer from the Merrill Herald newspaper stopped by. He took three pictures of the cider mill and one of the house, while the rest of us went about our work, Ardyce gave him the whole story while drinking iced tea in the shade of the front porch. Motioning me over, Ardyce had me give him the story on my father and how we found the deed. Mr. Fischer was fascinated by the entire story and promised a full page in the paper in a few days. I gave him a jug of cider as he was leaving.

"That story ought to sell every jug of cider we can squeeze out," Jake said with a big smile.

It is hard to describe the aroma of cider in the making. As the apples go through the crusher, the scent of autumn fills the air. It's sweet, tangy, almost sharp taste fills the nose and rolls over the tongue. I genuinely believe the reason people come to the mill to buy cider is as much for the experience of seeing and smelling the cider being pressed as for the cider itself. The blending of four varieties of apples, each with its distinct aroma, create a drink unlike any other.

Sheriff Melvin Hobart did indeed bring his girlfriend to see our new sign. As the police car drove slowly into the yard, Ardyce and I were waiting to greet them, and we got the surprise of our lives! Out of the car stepped Mrs. Lucy Baxter, owner of Baxter's motor Court where Ardyce and I had spent our first night in Merrill!

Melvin beamed a smile as he introduced us. "I know you already know this lovely lady," he said. "So, I don't need to introduce you. Mrs. Baxter is and has been a widow for over five years. I was lucky to have been a long-time friend of Peter, her late husband, who was a conductor on the railroad."

Melvin paused for a moment, lost in thought. "He, unfortunately, died of cancer. It was Luther who bought us back together, and we've been keeping what some call 'steady company' ever since."

From the mill came Luther's shout "Hi Dad, Hi Lucy! We're making cider!"

Lucy Baxter told us that the motor court was still doing business, although less than before the depression set in. "I probably get more people looking for work than people on vacation," she said with a sigh. "It just breaks your heart to see these families struggling to get by."

"I want to thank you for those families you sent here to work," Ardyce told her. "They really are a fine bunch of people."

With a slight frown, Lucy responded, "I try to pick out those who not only want to work but also those who seem to be responsible and honest folks."

"How is it that Luther brought you two together?" I asked Melvin.

Chuckling kind of to himself the sheriff said, "On Sundays, Luther and I sometimes take a drive just to talk and be together. About a month ago, we were headed out to Wolf Lake, and out of nowhere, Luther says, 'Let's stop and invite Mrs. Baxter along.' I couldn't think of a good reason not to, so we stopped. Lucy packed us a lunch and the three of us had a picnic."

"It was a wonderful day," Lucy chimed in. "I guess Melvin and I hadn't realized how lonely we were, but Luther sure did. That boy is the sweetest soul. It's like he knew we needed to be together."

That afternoon, as the happy couple drove away, Ardyce linked her arm through mine and whispered, "It is a comfort to know that two mature people can still find happiness."

"I wonder how Luther knew to bring them together?"

With a soft little laugh, Ardyce said, "Luther is a very sensitive young man at heart. If you asked him why, he would probably tell you 'because they belong together,' and he would be right."

Cider sales did pick up after the story and pictures in the newspaper. Families came with their cameras to have their photo taken under the sign. Often myself, Ardyce, Jake, and even Elmer and Luther were asked to pose with the families. Some would hold up jugs of cider as though drinking from them.

Dalton Fischer from the paper told us he could have labels made up for us and print them right at the newspaper. We ordered five hundred labels that we would later glue onto the jugs. In the back of my mind, I was already thinking of planting more apple trees. But what varieties of apples? Maybe more of the same? I planned to do more reading about it this winter.

CHAPTER FORTY-ONE

In 1931, the great depression settled in across America. Those living in small towns and on farms did not feel fortunate, but they were, due to one thing. Food. Anyone with a plot of land could at least grow a garden. Sometimes food was traded for labor. Farmers had chickens for eggs and cows for milk. Vegetables were the main meal in many small townhomes. Not so for large cities.

All across the land people living in cramped apartments in Chicago, New York, Kansas City, and Minneapolis were starving to death. The food riots began in Minneapolis. Meat markets, produce stores, grocery stores, and even restaurants were mobbed by starving people bent on getting food. In Detroit, the owner of a meat market was beaten and left for dead as his place of business was emptied of every last bit of meat. In Chicago, rioters were fired upon by police as they stormed a produce market. One police officer was injured and two rioters killed before order was restored.

The big gangster of the day, Alfonse Capone, opened six soup kitchens throughout Chicago to feed the hungry.

Cities in Iowa, Indiana, and Wisconsin met the same fate. In Milwaukee a crowd broke into a bakery, tied up the owner and two of his employees and cleaned out the bakery, taking bags of flour and sugar as they left. Children were often left at churches and orphanages because parents could no longer feed them. In New York City the mayor sent a flatbed truck out early every morning to pick up the bodies of the homeless who had died during the night from starvation. They were buried in unmarked graves outside the city. Boston did much the same thing as did Newark, New Jersey. 1932 promised no better as the money flow stalled to a trickle. Those wealthy enough hired guards to protect their property.

With a little effort, we got Mr. Winkelman's barrels filled with cider. Ardyce called to let his secretary know, and the next day a truck arrived to pick them up. Laying planks from the truck to the floor of the mill, three of us managed to roll the barrels up into the truck and stand them up. As the driver tied the barrels down, I filled a Red Wing jug with cider. Handing it to the driver, I told him, "This is a gift to Mr. Winkelman to thank him for his business."

"I will be sure to let him know," we were told. June had done a great job lettering the jugs. They looked like a professional had done the work.

The kitchen was a mess and smelled different from any canning operation. Lilly and Ardyce were stripping the outside leaves from the cabbages we had grown in the garden this summer.

"Lilly and I are going to make sauerkraut," Ardyce informed me. On the floor by the kitchen table was a five-gallon crock with a wooden cover that fits inside. On the table was a contraption I had never seen before.

Noticing my curiosity, Lilly said, "That is a kraut cutter

passed down to me from my mother." It was a wooden board about two foot long. In the middle, a hole had been cut, and three shiny metal blades set inside and screwed down. On top sat an open-ended wooden box.

Handing me a head of cabbage, Lilly said. "Put the cabbage in the box with the stem up and slide it over the blades." With very little effort the blades cut into the cabbage, shredding it into green confetti.

Both Ardyce and Lilly were laughing and exclaimed, "Set the cutter on the crock so that the kraut falls in!" I was hooked. I should have been taking care of business at the cider mill, and here I was cutting sauerkraut!

"Is that all there is to it?" I asked.

"Oh no, Aaron. To make the brine we add canning salt to a half-quart of water and pour it over the sliced cabbage." Lilly explained. "Then the wooden cover is used to pack the kraut down tight. You must set a gallon jug of water on the cover overnight to keep it packed down."

"How long does it take before it's actually sauerkraut?" I asked.

Thinking a minute, Lilly answered, "With five gallons of kraut it should sit for six weeks. Then we pack it into quart jars to store it."

Ardyce had that 'I'm a homemaker in training' look on her pretty face as she listened intently to every word from Lilly. I eased my way back outside and left them to their work.

On my way back to the barn, I met Jake. "Come winter, that sauerkraut will be real tasty," he said with a smile.

October is probably my favorite month of the year. The nights are cool, sometimes almost cold. The stars seem to glow with a special light, and when the harvest moon is in full phase the night never really gets dark. The days are warm without the sticky humidity of summer. The leaves on the oak, maple, and birch trees turn into colors mother nature never dreamed were possible. Even the garden added to the seasonal splendor: bright orange pumpkins, multi-colored squash, heads of green cabbage and carrot tops.

The fall flowers Ardyce had planted by the front porch gave their dainty but brilliant contribution. Dahlias, asters, begonias, coneflowers, and white daisies caught the eye each time I passed them. The sumac by the edge of the woodlot shone a dark red against the goldenrod in the field.

When the first hard frost came at the end of the month, much of this beauty would fade quickly to be replaced by the brown colors of dying plant life. As the Bible says 'to everything there is a season.' The meaning of it all is that no living thing passes through this world without some recognition. Plantlife, animal life, even the people around us are remembered separately and distinctly for what they bring to our lives daily.

CHAPTER FORTY-TWO

The morning dew wet my trouser cuffs as I walked the orchard. The sun was barely up, and the day would be starting soon. These early morning walks give me peace of mind as well as seeing for myself how much longer we had before the season was over. I estimated about a week, and the trees would be bare of apples. It had been a good year so far, with only eleven jugs left from the day before. Today, I would let Jake take over while I helped Ardyce bring in the last of the vegetables from the garden. The carrots were already harvested, but there were still the potatoes to dig, clean and store in the cellar. The pumpkins and squash were ready but could wait another few days.

The shelves in the cellar groaned under the weight of quart jars full of food waiting to take us through another winter. Ardyce and Lilly had also canned rabbit and made relish. June had her hands full watching the children and Sam. Their youngest, David, wasn't walking yet but could crawl as fast as I could walk. Tomorrow the ladies would be canning at Elmer and June's while Lilly got to babysit. The world would be a lonely place without good neighbors.

"Have you noticed Mildred seems to be attracted to Tom?" Ardyce whispered in my ear.

I thought about it for a moment and realized she was right! Mildred was a widow in her early 30's who sometimes dressed more like a man than a woman. Bib overalls and old flannel shirts were her usual uniform. Lately, this had changed. Summer blouses and jeans were more her style now. A new western-style straw hat had replaced the old sweat-stained slouch hat and yesterday, I'm sure I noticed her wearing lipstick. The change came gradually over several weeks so men would not have noticed, but women certainly would have. Now that Ardyce had pointed it out, I decided to quietly observe the reason for the change.

When Mildred drove up to the doors to unload the baskets of apples, she made sure she was at her best — straightening her blouse, checking her face in the truck's mirror and setting her hat at a jaunty angle. She would gently take hold of the basket to help Tom pour the apples into the waiting buckets. When Tom said, "Thanks, Mildred," she replied. "Call me Millie, everyone does."

Her sister Lottie, who was helping fill the jugs with cider, was watching and smiling to herself. Winks and nods were exchanged between the other women, but Tom seemed totally unaware. Hank was also watching the widow. He caught me watching him, smiled, and gave a little wink!

At lunchtime, Mildred shyly approached Tom. "I think I made more sandwiches than I can eat, would you like to join me?" she asked.

"I'll meet you on the bench outside the door after I wash up at the pump," he said.

Hank walked over to me, still smiling. "I think Tom has attracted a lady admirer."

"Will this interfere with your plans to work the logging camp this winter?" I asked.

Shaking his head, Hank said, "Tom isn't likely to settle down that quick. He will probably keep in touch with letters. Like me, traveling is in his blood, and it will take some time for him to decide to stay in one place."

I walked to the house, and there was Ardyce on the front porch watching Mildred and Tom. As they talked and ate, Mildred would occasionally lay her hand on his arm as she spoke. They both laughed at something, and Tom patted her knee. It was an age-old mating ritual that I had been through only recently.

As I sat down and tossed my hat on the porch, Ardyce smiled, and said, "As I watch those two, I remember a young man named Aaron going through the same motions on my folks front porch."

"I think I was more nervous than Tom," I said. "Probably because I had marriage on my mind."

"A few times, I felt you were going to ask me, but you didn't. Then finally one evening after we kissed you did ask, and I think my folks were in the house listening because when I told them, it was like they already knew."

"I was always a little afraid you would turn me down because Dad and I moved around so much."

"I knew when I first met you that you would be my husband and the father of my children," Ardyce said, patting my hand. "Now, eat your lunch."

The last truckload of apples was unloaded. The pickers followed carrying the ladders and poles. It was about two o'clock, and we still had to grind and press the last batch. Many helping hands unloaded the baskets under Mildred's watchful eye. The ladders and poles were stored in the barn, and as the baskets were emptied into the buckets, several of the pickers headed to their campsites to make supper and begin packing up. Business had been good all day with people waiting for their jugs of cider.

Twelve jugs of cider had been set aside: two jugs each for Jake and Elmer, two for Luther, two for Lucy Baxter and four jugs for Ardyce and I. I planned to let two of those ferment into hard cider for the holidays.

The printed labels donned the front of each jug and looked quite professional. Dalton Fischer had done an excellent job with white printing on a brown background surrounded by a gold border. Mr. Winkelman had been so impressed with the Red Wing jug he had sent us a five dollar gift certificate with a note expressing his pleasure. It had been a good harvest. I felt a deep satisfaction for a job well done and an affection for those who had done the work.

CHAPTER FORTY-THREE

Jake's woodlot had a lot of ash and beech trees ready to be turned into firewood. We had cut them down last year and let them dry out. We would do the same this year to be prepared for next year. Jake was cutting the limbs off while Elmer and I worked a two-person saw. Hank and Tom were splitting the bigger pieces and loading the truck.

"Time for lunch," Jake said, walking to his truck and setting down his axe. He opened the door, reached inside and hauled out a covered basket and a jug of water. "Lilly packed us a lunch, so pull up a log and let's eat,"

Shaking off the sawdust, we each found a spot to sit and waited as Jake uncovered the basket and passed it around. Chicken sandwiches on homemade bread, a jar of dill pickles and a package of oatmeal cookies. As we ate, we talked about Hank and Tom leaving for the logging camp.

"We should be on our way by next week if we want to get a good bunk," Tom said.

"How do you find out which ones are better than others?" Jake asked.

Taking a sip of water, Hank explained, "The best bunks are away from the door but close to the pot-bellied stove.

These are shotgun bunks, where you climb in from the foot of the bunk. All are double bunks, so a bottom bunk is better."

"Do they feed you good," Elmer asked.

"The cook is an older guy from Denmark who used to cook for a hotel," Tom said with a big smile. "His flapjacks are light as a feather. Platters of eggs and bacon and gallons of coffee to start the day. At noon the cook and his helper bring out lunch on a sled, which is usually hot beef sandwiches and more coffee. Then supper is always something different, like chicken or pork chops or maybe a big roast."

"At a logging camp, you get a good crew by how good the cook is," Hank said.

The rest of the afternoon, I thought about those flapjacks.

For the next week, we made firewood. Elmer's farm was next, and then we moved on to my place. We swapped wood back and forth. My woodlot had a lot of oak and maple while Elmer's woods ran to mostly elm and birch trees. We all ended up with a good blend of hardwoods plus some pine for cooking and kindling. All the chimneys had been cleaned in the spring by pulling a young pine tree up and down the chimney, knocking loose any build-up that could start a roof fire. Fresh tar was needed to seal around the base of the chimney where the heat had dried it out. It all was part of getting ready for winter. While we worked, Ardyce was busy washing and mending clothes for Hank and Tom. Mildred had knitted each a pair of socks. She and Tom had been keeping company lately, and we all wondered if the relationship would survive the separation. Tom promised to write and that they both would be back in the spring.

The first hard frost arrived on November 5th—the overnight temperature dropped to 18 degrees. I stoked the furnace about four in the morning to heat the house. There was frost on every windowpane in the kitchen as I put the coffee on to boil. I then stepped out on to the front porch in the morning darkness followed by Sam.

All the trees and bushes glowed white with a feather-like coating of frost. I could hear Sam walking on the frozen grass as he searched for just the right spot to relieve himself. Looking toward the barn, I was glad Elmer and I had bolted the plow back onto the REO truck. The Farmer's Almanac was predicting an early and snowy winter. The wood was cut, split and stacked in the cellar. When the snow arrived, we would be ready.

It's late evening. The sun is setting on the shores of Thunder Bay, Ontario, Canada. A seaplane is moored at the dock with its cargo bay door open. Men are loading cases of Canadian whiskey on board. Another seaplane, this one empty, is also moored there. It too will soon be loaded with whiskey. As the last case of whiskey is loaded, the cargo door is closed, and the plane moves out into the bay. The engines power-up, the plane slowly moves across the water gathering speed. In a spray of lake water, the plane rises into the night. Gaining altitude, it banks slightly to the right and is lost in the darkness of the night sky.

The pilot has made this trip many times before. He knows he is headed for Cranberry Lake outside the town of Couderay, Wisconsin. Cranberry Lake is a long straight forty-acre body of water.

On the shore of the lake sits a very well built home with thick stone walls, double glass windows, and heavy oak doors. Its owner is Alphonse Capone, the mob boss from Chicago, Illinois. For the next ten years, Mr. Capone will reside in federal prison after being convicted on tax evasion. Taking his place is Frank Nitti, his under-boss, now in control of Capone's entire empire.

Frank stands on the dock, the glowing red tip of his cigar winking in the dark. Far to the north, the faint drone of airplane engines is borne on the wind. Soon the small yellow lights in the dark sky do a circle of the lake, and the plane settles gently into the water. The headlights of two trucks waiting on shore light up the dock and the seaplane. The cargo door opens, and many hands begin carrying the cases of whiskey from the plane to the trucks.

They work quickly knowing another seaplane will be arriving in an hour. With the whiskey unloaded the plane taxi's to the end of the lake, takes off and is soon out of sight. The trucks move slowly out to the highway. Driving all night, they will be in Chicago by late afternoon.

CHAPTER FORTY-FOUR

"There are some pretty big deer tracks in the cut-over cornfield along with some smaller tracks; probably a buck and some does," Jake said.

Elmer and I were having coffee at Jake and Lilly's, talking over our plan for tomorrow's deer hunt.

"If one of us was to sit at the edge of the woodlot and the other two walk through it slowly from the back, I bet those deer would walk right out to the cornfield," Elmer said.

"You young fellers do the walkin', I'll do the sitting," Jake said, lighting his pipe.

I planned to hunt with Dad's 1903 Springfield, Elmer would carry his lever-action Model '94 Winchester. Jake was partial to his Savage Model 99 he had purchased new in 1900.

All three of us agreed to take only a buck. The deer herd was slowly coming back to northern Wisconsin, and we wanted to do our share to help rebuild it.

A three-quarter moon hung in the dark sky. It was five o'clock when I quietly left the house. A few inches of light snow had drifted down overnight, and the temperature showed at 21 degrees. The van started with no trouble, and I drove to Jake's, making fresh tire tracks on the snow-covered gravel road. Elmer was getting out of his truck when I parked by the house.

Lilly opened the door. "Come in and have some coffee and biscuits. Jake has already started."

Elmer and I shucked off our coats and sat down just as Lilly laid a platter of hot biscuits and a jar of honey on the table.

"If you two take Ranger Road, and park in the turn-around, it's only a quarter-mile across the hayfield to the back of my woodlot," Jake said as he slathered honey on another biscuit. Elmer and I both nodded with our mouths full of hot coffee. The three of us went through a dozen biscuits and a gallon of coffee.

We bundled into our coats and stepped into the moonlit yard. Jake set off across the field behind the machine shed as Elmer and I drove out of the yard.

A pale pink-yellow light announced the dawn. Elmer and I moved slowly across the field talking in whispers.

"Let's move real slow," Elmer said. "We don't want to scare them, just get them moving."

"If I get a good look at one, I'll take a shot," I told him.

"Better make it count, or dad will be really mad," he said with a little chuckle.

As we got to the treeline, Elmer moved left, and I went to the right. The woods were quiet, and the light snowfall muffled our footsteps. My eyes moved left to right and then back to the center. I stopped and listened but could only hear Elmer. A squirrel popped his head out of a hole in a big oak, saw me and went back in his den. Ahead I heard some movement in the brush. I stopped again but didn't see anything moving. About halfway into the woodlot, I looked over and saw Elmer pointing ahead.

BANG! BANG! It was Jake shooting! I waited a moment but didn't hear any more shots, so I pushed ahead.

BANG! Off to my left, Elmer shot! I could see Jake ahead of me, so I moved quickly up to where he was standing.

"Got a big buck down in the cornfield," said Jake. "Let's wait and see what Elmer shot at."

We heard Elmer yelling, "I got him!" Jake and I walked back into the woods and came on Elmer standing over a fat spike buck.

Looking at Jake, he said, "When you shot, this one turned to circle back and crossed right in front of me."

Elmer and I each grabbed a spike and dragged the buck out to Jake's stand. Jake walked out into the cornfield, picked up the blood trail, and followed it to the middle of the field.

He stopped and hollered, "Got a nice six-pointer here."

Elmer stripped off his coat, took out his hunting knife and began field-dressing his spike. Looking out in the cornfield I saw Jake do the same. Later Jake hauled both deer to the barn with the tractor. With a rope around the head, both were hauled up and tied off. The hides were peeled off, and both deer were quartered.

Lilly, June, and Ardyce would help us cut them up, wrap the meat and parcel it out. The venison would help us make it through another winter.

I was scratching my head as I went over the numbers and figures. I felt a hand on my shoulder, looked up, and saw Ardyce peering down at the ledger.

"How is it going?" she asked.

"As best as I can figure, we made $2,875 this year. Does that sound right to you?" I asked.

Patting me on the shoulder, she said, "With the expenses we had, like the labels and new baskets that sounds about right."

"For being in the middle of a depression, I guess we are doing better than average," I said. "Now I have to deduct taxes and Christmas expenses."

Elmer and June were hosting the Thanksgiving dinner this year. The women had the menu all planned. Ardyce would bring an apple pie, a pumpkin pie and a loaf of bread and I would bring a jug of hard cider. The roast came from the buck Jake got during hunting season, along with mashed potatoes, gravy, stewed tomatoes, raspberry jam, milk for the kids, and hot coffee later. It promised to be another glorious feast.

Their daughter, Francine, had recently gotten engaged to a young man named Edward Thorpe. She would be spending the day with her soon-to-be in-laws but would be home for Christmas. Elmer and I had mounted the plow on the REO truck the week before hunting season, and two snowfalls had kept him busy. No below zero days yet, but we all knew they were coming. A stock of well-seasoned wood was ready and waiting.

CHAPTER FORTY-FIVE

It was two weeks before Christmas, and I was sitting on the sofa having a morning cup of coffee, watching Reuben and Sam. They were laying on the bearskin rug by the fireplace. They had been playing since sunrise and were now napping in the sunlight coming in the living room window.

The phone rang, and Ardyce answered. Suddenly she was yelling. "Aaron, it's Jake! Harvey Lundgren's roof is on fire!"

I jammed my feet into my snow boots, grabbed my coat and cap, and ran for the door. The panel-van started on the first try, and I drove to the head of the drive. I heard the siren of the pumper fire-truck coming and waited till it passed, followed by Sheriff Hobart.

I stayed right behind them as the big fire-truck pulled as close to the house as possible. Ladders were propped against the eaves and men were swarming over the roof beating at the flames with wet burlap sacks.

Eldon Frye, the fire chief, was out of the truck before it came to a complete stop and started giving orders. "All you men get down from there so we can turn the hose on the fire. Everybody get off that roof now! Move it!"

Those on the roof clambered down, and the chief yelled, "clear!" Two men held the brass nozzle, and two more held the canvas hose as the water suddenly gushed forth. The thick black smoke slowly turned to a hazy grey, then began to dissolve into steam. The volume of water dropped away as the pumper ran dry. It had done its work, and the fire was out.

Men clambered back up the ladders checking for any burning embers. The roof was cedar shakes and tar-paper over pine boards, a firefighters nightmare. Any small pocket of heat could hold a tiny spark at its center and erupt when least expected.

Hammers and crowbars were passed up to the men as the chief told them to tear off anything charred no matter how small.

"Peel those shakes back at least two feet and check for ash," Chief Frye ordered.

Singed cedar shakes and charred pine boards rained down to the men below who piled them to one side away from the house.

"All the roof struts are in good shape," one of the firemen called down. "We put the fire out before it got through."

Old Harvey Lundgren sat on an upturned bucket with his head in his hands, tears slowly dripping down between his knees. His son Adam patted his Dad's back. "It'll be alright, Pa, we can fix it," he said softly, over and over.

As the firemen rolled up the hoses and laid them back on the truck, Eldon removed his helmet, pulled a five-dollar bill from his pocket and dropped it in. He handed the helmet to one of his men saying, "Pass this around. Harvey is going to need some lumber."

Every man there gave something. I put in a ten-dollar bill, Jake and Elmer both gave a five. The helmet was given back to Chief Frye. He folded the bills together, knelt in front of Harvey and pressed the wad of bills into the man's hand.

"Harvey, you have enough here to buy boards and shakes to fix that roof. Now stop the crying and get over to the sawmill."

The chief then stood up and looked around the crowd. "Who has a truck big enough to haul a load of lumber?"

Elmer stepped forward. "The REO plow truck can handle it." He looked at me, and I nodded. Adam got Harvey into the truck. Elmer backed it around and drove away.

"All you men who have hammers, saws, and nails go get them," Jake said. "Meet back here in an hour. By dark, we can have a good start on covering that hole."

I went home to get my tools. Elmer's pickup truck was in the yard. As I walked into the house, the smell of fresh coffee filled the air.

In the kitchen, Lilly, Ardyce, and June were filling a box with sandwiches. Three jugs of hot coffee sat on the table, ready to go.

"June will stay with the children," Lilly said, handing me a cup of coffee. "Your wife and I will be there directly with coffee and food."

A quick glance at the wall clock showed it was almost noon. We would have about five hours of daylight to get the boards on the roof. The shingles would have to wait until tomorrow.

"I will leave you the panel-van and take Elmer's pickup," I told Lilly. A quick kiss for my wife, a hug for Reuben and a head scratch for Sam, then I was back out the door.

We nailed on the last two roof boards by the light of a lantern. Gus Fricke at the sawmill had estimated how many boards we would need. We had one six-footer left over. The bundles of cedar shakes and a roll of tar-paper were stacked on the porch, ready to be nailed on tomorrow.

The sandwiches and coffee had disappeared during the afternoon. Two men had taken the time to pull the nails from the burned boards and shakes, many of which we had reused. That wood would be added to the woodpile and be burned for fuel. Nothing went to waste during this depression.

Harvey, his wife Alma and son Adam, made the rounds shaking everyone's hand and thanking them for the help. We all knew it could have been any one of us in need of a helping hand.

By two in the afternoon of the next day, the roof was done. A half bundle of shakes was all that was left over. It looked a bit strange with the new and old shakes together, but soon time and weather would do its work. Although some water had come through leaving two water stains on the ceiling, it was a job well done by good neighbors.

CHAPTER FORTY-SIX

Christmas dinner was at our house this year, and Ardyce had the house ready. We opened our presents early Christmas morning. Our trip to Winkelman's a week earlier had been primarily for things we needed rather than things we wanted. A few decorations, some yarn, more colored thread, a bolt of cotton, leather gloves, kitchen spices, along with flour and sugar, and some small presents for our guests made up the list.

The Singer sewing machine had kept up a steady clatter. When it was silent, the *click, click, click* of knitting needles took its place. Reuben and I spent those afternoons grooming Sam and building forts from wooden blocks. Sam's tail was the enemy, and his aim was very good. The blocks would tumble, Reuben would laugh and clap his little hands.

I made a large pine-bough wreath that Ardyce decorated with bows and small ornaments. It hung over the fireplace, adding the aroma of fresh-cut pine to the smell of delicious things coming from the kitchen.

The Jenske brothers had come through with an apple-wood smoked ham. Lilly, Jake, Francine and Edward, and Elmer and June, with the children Louise and David, would complete our Christmas gathering. The table would be groaning under the weight of the food. My last jug of hard cider would be uncorked and enjoyed. Small gifts would be given and received with much oohing and aahing from the ladies. Sam would be overfed with bits of ham from willing hands. The small candles on the Christmas tree would be lit much to the delight of the children. We would all relax before the fire remembering the events of the past year.

After goodbyes were said, the food would be put away, and the kitchen cleaned up. Reuben would be put to bed, then my lovely wife and I would enjoy some together time before banking the fire and making our way to bed.

On the morning of January 5th, 1933, Franklin and Gretta Murfeld burned down their house and small barn. Their one-hundred-acre farm located just north of the crossroads community of Gilbert had been foreclosed on by the bank in Merrill. The Murfeld's, both in their early thirties with no children, had already sold off the livestock, farm equipment and anything else of value to keep food on the table.

They owned two things. A Model T Ford with bald tires and a Winchester pump shotgun. What little food and clothing they had left was piled in the backseat of the Ford. The buildings were old and weathered and within two hours were burned to the foundations. Without a word, they got into the Model T and drove to Merrill.

Bank President Giles Newcombe lived in a two-story house mail-ordered from Sears & Roebuck years ago by

Giles' father. It sat on a half-acre of land almost at the end of Perkins street. Giles was at home having lunch with his wife Nancy when the Murfeld's Ford parked in their drive. Without bothering to knock, Franklin entered the front door carrying the shotgun. He ordered the Newcombe's out of the house and had them stand in the drive. Handing the shotgun to Gretta, he lifted a gallon can of gasoline from the Ford and re-entered the house. When he came back out minutes later, the can was empty, and smoke was coming from the open doorway.

"This is how it feels to have no home," he said to Giles. As the flames began to poke through the roof, Franklin and Gretta got in the Ford, backed it around and drove away. They were arrested by the State Patrol north of Wausau without incident. Both were given a five-year prison sentence.

Today, the temperature was seven below zero. It hadn't varied a lot over the past three days except to drop lower at night. The sun, hanging like an ornament under a clear blue sky, gave no warmth.

I was in the cellar feeding wood into the furnace, thankful the supply of split hardwood was plentiful.

Last fall, Jake had warned, "Haven't had a really cold winter in some time, this could be the year."

Using this wisdom, I had added another stack to the usual amount. Closing the furnace door, I turned and started back to the stairs. Taking two steps, I tripped! Looking down I saw one of the fieldstones in the floor had a corner poking up.

'Frost heave,' I thought to myself.

With the heel of my boot, I pushed down on the stone. It moved slightly but not all the way down. Unlike most of the other stone flooring, this stone was almost square. Once again, I pushed down on the stone, and this time, I heard a muffled 'clink.' Now my curiosity was aroused.

I knelt and looked closely at the stone. There was very little mortar. There was no way to lift the stone out, it was about eighteen inches square, and I couldn't guess how deep it was set. Realizing this would require some tools, I made a quick trip to the kitchen pantry where I kept basic tools for home repairs.

Choosing a hammer and screwdriver, I was back in the cellar within minutes. Carefully tapping the screwdriver down along the side of the raised corner, I slowly eased the edge of the stone up. As the raised corner shifted, the side I was levering on, came free. I slid my fingers under the stone and lifted.

The stone was five inches thick and heavy. Carefully sliding the stone toward me, I laid it off to the side. Underneath, a square hole slightly smaller than the top stone, and inside was a metal box about a foot square with a handle on top.

Raising the handle, I lifted the box out of the hole. It was heavy and cold from being in the ground. I picked it up and took it upstairs.

"Ardyce, come and see what I found!" As I set the box down on the rug in front of the sofa, Ardyce came from the kitchen, wiping her hands on her apron.

Staring at the box in wonder, she asked, "Where did you find that?" I told her about the stone in the cellar floor.

"The frost in the ground must have pushed up just enough to unseat the one corner," I said.

Sitting down on the sofa next to me, she asked, "Are you going to open it or just look at it?"

There was no lock on the box, just a metal latch. I popped it open and lifted the lid. On the top was a square bundle wrapped in heavy cloth and tied with a cord. Carefully removing the cord, I unwrapped the package. Inside were old pictures, letters, and documents.

Picking up the pictures, Ardyce exclaimed, "These must be pictures of Dieter and his family." There were six pictures in all. One of Dieter and his wife, two of them with a baby, two more with the children about age three and again maybe age ten; another photo was of a young man in an Army uniform and the last of another young man standing by the cider press. Some of the older letters were written in what appeared to be German, some postmarked from France, probably written by Einar before he was killed in the war, and some from the U.S. Army.

The documents were varied. A wedding certificate in German, two birth certificates, two baptism certificates, tax bills marked PAID, the title for the house and land and a title for the REO truck. At the bottom of the box was a thick leather pouch with straps and buckles. This was why the box was so heavy. I lifted out the pouch, closed the lid on the box, and laid the leather pouch on top. Undoing the straps, I reached inside and pulled out a wooden cigar box with a small metal clasp. I snapped the clasp open and lifted the cover.

"Oh my God, Aaron," Ardyce gasped. We were staring at rows of gold coins! I lifted one out and saw it was a twenty-dollar gold piece. There were five rows of coins with ten coins per roll. A thousand dollars in gold! I was speechless!

I don't know how long Ardyce and I sat and stared at the gold coins softly glowing in the sunlight coming through the window. It was Reuben's calling as he awoke from his nap that finally broke us out of our trance.

"What do we do now?" Ardyce asked.

"We save all the pictures and documents. It's the story of a family's life and death that needs to be preserved. The gold will be used to keep the house in shape. A new kitchen range, a new roof on the house, things that Dieter would have done if he were here."

With tears in her eyes, Ardyce hugged me. "Me up! Me up!" Reuben hollered, which started Sam barking. The spell broken, life returned to normal. The extra money would ensure a stable future for my family. I put the coins away and went to put the fieldstone back over the hole in the cellar.

We told Jake and Lilly about the box and showed them the pictures.

"It sure explains a lot," Jake said. "When they came to sell off the furniture they couldn't find any of this stuff."

"I'll bet the museum in Merrill would like to have the pictures and documents," Lilly said.

"That's a wonderful idea," Ardyce agreed.

I led Jake down to the cellar and showed him the stone covering the hole.

"Might want to use that in the future" Jake mused.

"I'm using it now," I said with a smile.

CHAPTER FORTY-SEVEN

The middle of February can bring on the feeling of cabin fever. The same routine day after day trapped in the house. Winter is a necessary time of year. It gives the earth the moisture it will need for growth in the spring. It can also be tedious without the warmth of the sun or the warm breeze of a summer day.

Ardyce and I were looking forward to a night out. Two weeks before, we had been babysitting for Elmer and June's children. They had gone to a winter social gathering at the church. Now, it was our turn. They would take care of Reuben and Sam while Ardyce and I went to dinner and a movie.

"Something warm but dressy," I heard Ardyce mutter to herself. Her slender figure made almost anything look good, but this was a special night. No suit for me, just dress pants and white shirt, maybe a vest. A night on the town would do us both good.

The movie was a Laurel and Hardy comedy called 'Pack up your troubles.' These two natural comedians always gave us a good laugh. Later we drove to the Bristol Hotel. Their dining room was the finest in our area. The small chandeliers glowed brightly over tables covered with blinding white tablecloths. The plush chairs and thick carpet were an invitation to relax and enjoy the atmosphere. I swear the waiter snapped his heels together and bowed as he handed us the menus encased in a leather folder.

Ardyce gazed at the menu, looked over the top at me and whispered, "I already know what I want, but I can't decide on a dessert."

"I'll pick a dessert and surprise you," I whispered back.

We had lobster. It was expensive and delicious. A delicate white wine went well with the meal. As the waiter approached, I beckoned him to lean over and whispered in his ear. He smiled and nodded and clicked his heels again. Minutes later he returned with a covered dish. Setting it on the table, he lifted the lid.

Ardyce gasped, giggled and in a squealy voice said, "Strawberry shortcake! It's perfect!"

On the way home, my wife cuddled close. "Thank you for a wonderful night out I will remember for years," she breathed in my ear.

"It was an honor to be the escort for the most beautiful lady in the room," I told her. I felt completely content, having spent the perfect evening with the love of my life.

March blew in with two feet of snow. No significant wind or howling blizzard, just a steady snowfall that lasted a day and a half. The temperature held steady at twenty-five degrees night and day. I shoveled the path to the barn to gather eggs and feed the chickens. About ten o'clock the next morning, Elmer drove in and plowed the drive. I stepped out on the porch and waved him in for some hot coffee. He shucked off his coat and sat down just as Ardyce handed him a steaming mug.

"Nothing moving out there but me," he said with a big grin. The REO truck was making him a little more money this year. Lincoln County had given him the contract to plow out Wolf Creek Road. The road ran for six miles before it hooked up with the county trunk. Elmer and I shared all repairs and tune-ups for the truck during the winter, but so far things were running smoothly.

By the middle of March, the day time temperature hovered between forty and fifty, then dropped into the twenties at night.

"It's time to tap that grove of sugar maples in your woodlot," Jake informed me.

I had never done this and was looking forward to making our own maple syrup. Jake and Elmer arrived at daybreak with Jake's pickup truck holding everything we would need. An auger to tap the trees with, a hammer, metal taps to set in the trees, buckets to catch the sap and a huge cast-iron cauldron to boil down the sap into syrup. The pot stood on sturdy legs about six inches off the ground. We hauled it all out to the maple grove and set up.

"You got to be careful not to tap too deeply into the tree," Jake said. "If you tap into the heartwood you get no sap and maybe lose the tree."

The auger drilled into the maple at a slightly upward angle so the sap would run down. With a few good blows from the hammer the tap was driven into the hole, and a gallon bucket was hung on it. We tapped two dozen trees.

"If we need more, then we tap more," Elmer told me. The sap made a steady plinking sound as it dripped into the buckets.

"When they get about half-full we pour them into the cauldron and boil off the excess fluid," Jake said. While the buckets were filling, we dug a wide shallow hole and set the big cauldron over it. Seasoned wood was gathered, and a fire started under the cauldron.

"It's important we keep the heat at an even level so as not to scorch the sap," Elmer said. "A good bed of hot coals works best."

As the cauldron heated, we began gathering some of the buckets that were filling and replacing them with empties. I slowly poured the first half-full bucket of sap into the heated cauldron. The aroma that drifted up was a sweet delight. Jake used a long-handled ladle with a wire mesh basket to skim off the frothy foam that gathered on the top of the sap.

"How do you know when it's syrup?" I asked.

With a knowing smile, Jake flipped the foam from the ladle onto the ground, saying, "As the sap boils down it will turn an amber color and thicken. Then we dip it out into quart jars. That's when it's syrup." The image of a stack of buttermilk pancakes drowning in home-made maple syrup fixed in my mind.

By the first of April, we pulled the taps from the trees, gathered the buckets, and boiled out the last batch of syrup. There was enough for all three families to enjoy the bounty. We poured the final syrup into jars, capped them and set them into the wooden box filled with straw. The snow was shoveled under the cauldron putting out the hot coals. The pot would sit for a few days to cool off then be scrubbed out and stored in Jake's shed until next year. Within a month the holes in the trees would grow over with no outward sign they had even been tapped.

The days were warming up, and buds could be seen on the trees. Cold nights still hung around, but the sun was a constant daytime companion. Spring in northern Wisconsin takes it time coming. It slowly eases winter out with gentle nudges of fifty degree days. Soft south-western breezes replaced the north-east winds. The geese drifted in with uneven V-formations, and the robins flitted about gathering anything usable for their nests. The wild rabbits were turning brown again, and the owls called at night. At the edge of our property, Wolf Creek flowed freely, no longer trapped in the ice that had held it in a wintry grip.

Windows could be opened to air out houses from the smell of wood-smoke and wet wool. Work gloves replaced mittens for warmth while heavy winter coats hung unused in the entryway. The buckets of ashes that had been stored in the barn were spread over the garden plot where spring rains would ease the needed potash into the soil. Clotheslines again hung with drying clothes that when worn, made you occasionally hold the cloth to your nose to breathe in the scent of spring. The wild asparagus would soon be sprouting in the ditches along Wolf Creek Road waiting for the discerning eye and steady hand of the housewife who knew where to look. No season gives more promise than spring.

CHAPTER FORTY-EIGHT

At the far end of Wolf Creek Road, just before it connects with the county trunk, one of the oldest farms in Lincoln County covers two-hundred-forty acres. It is owned by Rodney and Martha Woldt. The Woldt's have two children, Bruce age twelve and Linda, age ten. Rodney's widowed father, Jerome, lives with them. When Jerome's wife died, he signed the farm over to Rodney, his only child. Working together, the father and son now milked a small herd of eighteen Jersey cows.

The market crash had driven the price of milk so low it hardly paid to milk each day. The market price of corn and wheat was less than the cost of the seed. To survive in this atmosphere, a farmer needed a second source of income. The Woldt's had only the farm and the cows. Rodney had gotten a notice from the bank last week that foreclosure proceedings were in the works. In the spring of 1929, Rodney had borrowed $500 from the bank to purchase another good used tractor, a three-point plow, and a second-hand three-row corn harvester. The bank now wanted the loan paid.

"To settle the outstanding debt, your cattle and all machinery will be auctioned off" was the main content of the bank notice. The land was clear of debt, but the cows and all the machines it took to run it had been used as collateral on the loan. A notice of foreclosure was advertised in the newspaper. It looked like the Woldt farm would soon be out of business.

The auction would be held on Saturday morning. Thursday afternoon Jake and Lilly stopped to visit. We hadn't seen much of Jake for the last week and a half.

"I have been kinda busy driving around the county," Jake informed us.

Knowing he wasn't one to make social calls, I asked, "Are you planning to run for a seat on the town board?" I half expected a smile or at least a laugh, but I got neither.

"I need a big favor from you and Ardyce. Come to the auction at Rodney's on Saturday and bring about twenty dollars in singles and any spare change."

Then it dawned on me what Jake had in mind. "I'll be there early and help you. I think it's a great idea," I said.

Six o'clock on Saturday morning, I downed the last of my coffee, kissed Ardyce goodbye and left. I was anxious yet excited, knowing what was going to happen. Sheriff Hobart's police car was parked at the driveway entrance to the Woldt's farm. He and his son Luther waved me in.

I parked next to Elmer's truck, got out, and looked around. I spotted Jake slowly walking through the small crowd.

"Take a walk with me," Jake said quietly. Looking toward the driveway, I saw a flatbed truck being turned away. "This auction is going to be for family and friends only," Jake said. "No cattle buyers or machinery dealers are welcome."

By seven o'clock the auctioneer arrived with the banker. Jake and I made our way through the gathering shaking hands. Each handshake passed a dollar bill to those who didn't have any cash. A nod and a wink and sometimes a whispered 'thanks' followed. At eight o'clock sharp, the auctioneer rapped his gavel, and the auction began.

"You all know why we are here, so let's get started," the auctioneer hollered. His red suspenders held up black pants over a portly belly straining the buttons on his white shirt. "First up is this fine herd of Jersey cows. All eighteen are good milkers and will make a fine addition to any herd. Who will start the bidding?"

Abel Simms thrust his hand in the air and, in a loud, clear voice, said, "I'll bid a nickel apiece for them cows." The auctioneer's jaw dropped open, and his fleshy face turned pink.

"That's ridiculous! That's only ninety cents for the whole bunch! I can't accept a bid that low. Do I hear any more bids!"

Lester Bromley stepped out saying, "I'll make it an even dollar."

The auctioneer's face was now red. "These Jersey cows are worth at least $25 apiece! Do I hear any more bids!"

The banker was now on his feet, shaking his fist at the crowd. "You can't do this! The bank has a right to get its money back. Now let's hear some serious bids!" Nobody laughed, but a lot of people were smiling.

Jake stepped forward and pointed his pipe at the auctioneer. "You got a serious bid of one dollar," he said. "You best take it and get on with this auction." Seeing what he was up against the auctioneer lost some of the red in his face and banged his gavel.

"Sold to Mr. Bromley for one dollar." The banker now knew what was happening. The newspapers had been calling them 'penny auctions.' They were closed to outsiders. The banks were forced to accept the proceeds from the auction as settlement for the debt owed. Dabbing at his face with a handkerchief, the banker sank slowly back into his chair. The auctioneer had no choice but to continue.

The two tractors sold for a dollar apiece. Fifty cents for a plow, 25 cents for a hay-wagon, 75 cents for the three-row corn picker. As each item was offered someone bid 25 cents, another bid 50 cents and so on — not one thing sold for more than a dollar. The auctioneer was no longer hollering. The banker was on the verge of tears. The crowd was quiet and orderly with a firm resolve. With a final bang of his gavel, the auctioneer declared the auction over. Everyone who had their bid accepted stepped forward and paid. The banker counted the proceeds. $17.50 was the final tally. The auctioneer would receive a percentage of that total.

The banker and auctioneer were the first to leave. As they drove away, Luther stood at the end of the drive waving goodbye. The Woldt's were stunned! They had not been told what was going to happen. As the crowd began leaving each person who had purchased something stopped to shake hands with Rodney and Jerome.

"Don't need them cows right now, you just keep milking them," Lester Bromley told them.

"Got enough, tractors. You need them, I don't," said another.

"Didn't plant corn this year. I'll just leave that picker here," from a third. Not one thing left the farm.

On the way to their cars, these farmers also stopped to shake hands with Jake and me. Any dollar bills left over were passed back to us.

When the last car had left, Rodney and Jerome came forward. "We can never thank you enough for what you did," said Rodney.

"No need for that," Jake said. "Just helping out a neighbor."

Soon after, foreclosures stopped. The banks concluded that payments could be deferred as long as the farms continued to operate. A working farm kept the hope alive of someday getting their money back. It was a bare existence, but still an existence. Someday the nation would and must recover. Until then we all went about the business of day-to-day living.

The soft rain of late April made the world green overnight. The leaves on the trees, the grass, even the tiny flowers pushing their way through the damp soil. In the distance, the muted 'clank' of cowbells told of herds that had been closed in all winter now roaming pastures growing as fast as they could be eaten. It was the season of growth, of renewal, of sunshine and warm winds.

CHAPTER FORTY-NINE

WOOF! WOOF! Sam was barking at the door. His tail was almost spinning around, and it looked like he had a smile on his face! The month of May had arrived over the weekend, and I suspected we had company. Opening the door, I stepped out in time to see Sam with his front paws on Hank's shoulders licking his laughing face.

"Get down, Sam. Let the man have his coffee," Ardyce followed me out with Reuben right behind. Holding his arms up, Reuben cried, "Up Hank, lift me up!"

Hank lifted him, swung him around, and set him down. Ardyce handed us both a mug of hot coffee.

Looking around, I asked, "Where is Tom?"

With a big grin, Hank answered, "Tom is still in Merrill. He stopped to see Mildred."

With a knowing smile, Ardyce asked, "Is this getting serious for them?"

Smiling, Hank replied, "Tom is happy with the friendship, but a slow mover when it comes settling down. So far, Millie is alright with the way things are. Tom should be along tomorrow."

"How did the log drive go this spring?" I asked.

Frowning a bit, Hank said, "We lost one young man during a logjam. He tried to break it up with a peavey, which almost worked. When the log he was on rolled, he went under, and the whole thing came crashing down on him. We found him the next day a mile down-river." Taking a sip of coffee, Hank added, "Tom and I are thinking about joining that new CCC camp that's started ten miles northwest of here off Highway 107. The pay will be better, and we still will be cutting trees."

We had a new President this year, Mr. Franklin Roosevelt, who promised to drive away the dark cloud that has hung over the nation since 1929. It was decided that putting young men back to work was essential to getting the country back on track.

The Civilian Conservation Corps was established in April of 1933. Over two hundred sites in Wisconsin were chosen as camp bases. The men cleared the sites and built their bunkhouses, storage sheds, kitchens, mess halls, and offices. For their work, they would be paid $30 per month and issued surplus WWI uniforms as clothing and footwear. If the men were married, $25 from their pay was sent to their family. The plan was all-encompassing. They would build roads, bridges, dams, and parks, fight fires, layout and clear hiking trails, establish summer and winter recreational areas and maintain what had been built. It was a grand plan that everyone hoped would work.

With a twinge of apprehension, I asked Hank, "When do you and Tom think you will join up?"

With a twinkle in his eye, Hank answered, "Probably after the cider is made and the winter wood is cut."

Feeling I could breathe again, I said, "That is some good news. I don't suppose my wife's cooking has anything to do with your decision?"

Laughing now, Hank replied, "It was Ardyce's cooking and the free cider that made up our minds!"

Tom arrived the next day as spring house cleaning was already underway. The kitchen was given special attention. The old Blue Bird cookstove was being retired. Elmer, Hank, Tom and I took down the old stovepipe, removed the warming oven on top and slowly and carefully carried the cast-iron monster out the kitchen door to the barn. The walls, floor, and even the ceiling were scrubbed down to remove any trace of soot.

As we were finishing mopping the floor the telephone rang. It was Simms Hardware Store in Merrill letting us know the new stove had just arrived. Ardyce told them we would pick it up tomorrow morning.

The new stove was a South Bend model that Ardyce had chosen after much mental anguish over which stove was the best for us. Two warming ovens on top, a lined water reservoir and four top lids, two large and two smaller. Joe Simms and his son Donald helped us load the large wooden crate onto the truck and tie it down. After a cautious drive home, I backed the truck up to the kitchen door. Setting the container on the ground, we got the hammer and a crowbar and with great care took the crate apart.

The stove was a thing of beauty. A light tan color with black accents, it actually glowed in the sunlight. Three sections of new stove pipe came with it. Under the direction of my wife, we finally got the stove positioned and attached the new pipe sections. It was a little bigger than the old stove but still, fit nicely in the large kitchen.

Ardyce sat at the kitchen table, dabbing at her eyes with her apron.

"Is something wrong?" I asked.

Looking up with a teary smile, she said softly, "No, Aaron, everything is just perfect."

As a special thank you that night Ardyce made venison stew, using the last of the canned venison. For this treat, I would have rearranged the entire house. Reuben ate almost as much stew as I did. Sam lay on the rug hoping for any leftovers. Hank and Tom stopped eating at times to compliment Ardyce on the stew.

While I helped clear the dishes, Ardyce dished up a big slice of apple pie for everyone. I managed to finish the pie with a little room left for coffee. Sam got a small bowl of leftovers, and the stew was history.

CHAPTER FIFTY

In 1897, the State of Wisconsin purchased two hundred acres of land in Green Bay. The old brick factory on this site had once manufactured bicycles. Over time, the building was slowly renovated into a Reformatory for young men ages seventeen to twenty-four.

In 1930 an eighteen-year-old named Wilford 'Willie' Lange was arrested and sentenced to three years at the Reformatory for assault and robbery. His victim was a shoe store owner who tried to stop Willie from stealing a pair of boots. Running out of the store with a boot in each hand, Willie ran into a police officer about to enter the store. He was not a model prisoner but managed to do his time without any major incidents.

Willie was released in June of 1933 and began walking northwest. He planned to make it to Hibbing, Minnesota where his Uncle Bob owned a gas station. By eleven that night Willie came to Graff's Roadhouse. The parking lot was about half-full of cars and trucks. Willie chose a Studebaker with a cracked rear window and bald tires. In the glove box were a road map and a Smith & Wesson .38 revolver. He now had all a young man needed to succeed in life.

By morning Willie was in Shawano where a Standard gas station was just opening for business. After filling the tank, Willie robbed the owner, tied him up, and drove away. Outside of Tomahawk one of the bald tires blew out. Leaving the car on the side of the road Willie walked into town.

It was late evening when a man drove up and parked outside a drug store. The man left the motor of his red Desoto coupe running and went inside. Willie hopped in and drove away. Another gas station outside of town, another full tank and another robbery would get Willie to Hayward where his luck would run out.

By now the State police had been alerted and were looking for the red Desoto. Hungry and tired, Willie stopped at a diner just before Hayward. While he was eating, a State police car carrying two troopers drove by, saw the red coupe, and stopped to check it out. Willie finished eating, paid his bill, and walked outside, right into two shotguns held by two nervous troopers. Willie would spend the next seven years in prison, wondering where he went wrong.

Each spring seemed to bring some of nature's creatures to our orchard. This year it was squirrels. Elmer and I spent a few hours each day roaming the orchard with our .22's decreasing the squirrel population. Fortunately, they made a very tasty meal. We saved the tails because Jake told us, "Old Cooney will give you a penny apiece for them."

The apple trees were in full bloom, and the bees were constantly moving from one tree to the next. We knew there had to be a bee tree somewhere close by, but we had not found it yet.

We had eaten four chickens over the winter and Ardyce had three hens sitting on their nests waiting to hatch about a dozen more. One morning I saw tracks around the wire fence too small to be from Sam.

Jake came over to take a look and said, "Probably a fox. Looks like the same tracks I saw around my rabbit pens."

Cooney came out to look and said, "Them's fox tracks by golly. I'll set a trap at both places and catch them. A fox pelt with a good tail is worth five dollars." In all, four traps were set and took home two foxes and the biggest raccoon I have ever seen. He got it at Jake's farm and showed it to everyone on Wolf Creek road.

Jake and old Ned had plowed and diced the garden plot, and the first rows of vegetables were now in the ground. Carrots, onions, green beans, cucumbers, potatoes, yellow beans, and tomato seedlings that had been started early. Today the corn, squash, pumpkins, rutabagas, watermelons, and cabbage would join them. Last year we had made a scarecrow to keep the crows out but that only served as a place for the birds to land and perch on before the raid. What kept the crows at bay was Sam. If Sam were outside, the crows would move on. The rabbits also seemed to respect the garden as Sam's personal property and kept their distance. I often watched Sam walk between the rows sniffing the ground and checking the sky, with Reuben following along behind.

The roofers arrived in late May. Arnie Flack and his two sons, Chester and Nick, unloaded ladders and climbed up to give me an estimate on a new metal roof. The two sons climbed the ladders and roamed over the roof calling down numbers to Arnie, who wrote them in a notebook. After about twenty minutes, Nick and Chester climbed down, put the ladders away, and conferred with Arnie. There was some head shaking, some arm gestures, and intense whispering. Finally, all three agreed on something, and the discussion was over. Thumbing his battered fedora back on his balding head, Arnie smiled and gave me the news. "We can put that metal roof on for $275. An asphalt shingle job would only cost $100. Are you sure you want metal?"

"Have you ever done a metal roof on a house before?" I asked.

"Yessir, we did," Arnie replied. "That big Dupree house in Merrill. We have to order all the roofing pre-cut from a company in Milwaukee and have it shipped in by rail. That's why it costs more."

"How long will it take to do the job, and when can you start?" I asked.

With a smile, Arnie told me, "I can order it today. It will take a week to cut the panels, two days to get it here by train. While we are waiting, we can take the old cedar shakes off and lay down the tar-paper. Should have your new roof on by the second week in June." Arnie and I shook on the deal. I gave him $150 to pay his supplier and got a receipt. The rest would be paid when the job was done.

Tarpaulins covered the ground all around the house. "Don't want no nails or big splinters hiding in the grass," Arnie told me. The roof boards were in good shape. None needed replacing. Fresh tar was applied around the chimney and the cookstove pipe. The thick black tar-paper was laid down and tacked in place. The tarps full of old roofing and nails were bundled up, tied and lifted onto the back of Arnie's truck to be hauled away.

Two days later, Arnie and sons arrived at eight o'clock in the morning with the new roof. The heavy metal panels had been painted a dark green color and measured about three by eight-foot. The ladders were set up, and Chester and Nick climbed up with a coil of rope each.

Hank and Tom helped Arnie take the panels off of his truck one at a time. Each one was carried to the ladders where the ropes were waiting. Tying a line to each end of the metal roofing Arnie gave a wave of his hand, and the panel slid up the ladders. Chester and Nick untied the panel, carried it to the peak and nailed it down. This process would be repeated many times over the next few days until the roof was covered.

The roof cap was several half-round pieces already cut to size. Arnie's measurements had been right on the mark. When the job was done, there were no pieces left over. I paid Arnie, shook his hand for a job well done, and told him to drop by this fall for a free jug of cider.

CHAPTER FIFTY-ONE

Wolf Creek road was getting a new bridge! The old wooden, one-lane bridge would be replaced with a two-lane steel and plank structure designed and built by the CCC camp. It would take about a month to construct, and traffic would have to detour around by the County trunk road. When the bridge was completed, the road would be widened, graded, and re-graveled. When this was done Ardyce and I intended to have our driveway widened and a parking area added.

The smell of new-mown hay filled the air all along Wolf Creek road. We were putting up the first crop at Elmer's farm. The chain-driven hayloader steadily lifted the hay from the field to the wagon. Jake drove the tractor while Elmer and I spread the hay beneath our feet. When the load on the wagon was as high as the loader, Jake would haul it to the barn where Hank and Tom were waiting. The winter snow-melt and spring rains had done their work, and the tall lush grass had been cut and left to dry. After being raked and turned, it was ready for harvesting.

"Full load, Dad!" Elmer hollered. The wagon was unhooked, the loader pulled forward and unhooked, then the wagon hooked to the tractor for the trip to the barn.

As the last load of the day was being hauled up and into the hayloft, Lilly came from the house with a pitcher of iced tea and a tray of glasses. Draining half his glass Jake packed and lit his pipe.

"My first crop is already cut and raked, so we can start on that tomorrow," he said. Hank and Tom emerged from the barn wiping away the sweat with new blue kerchiefs.

Elmer joined us and asked Tom, "Any luck tracking down that bee tree yet?"

Tom had been trying to find the tree where the bees had settled on for their honeycomb.

Taking a big gulp of tea, Tom said, "I have it down to a general area. Now I have to get it down to a single tree." We were all hoping he would find that tree by fall.

Jake had a smoker that would calm the bees down and let us get the honeycomb out of the tree. Between the clover in the field and the apple blossoms, it would be the sweetest honey ever tasted.

Nothing says summer like the first strawberries. Lilly had a strawberry patch at the east end of her garden. She had given Ardyce some seedlings two years ago, and this year the big red berries were the size of my thumb! Ardyce and June were busy making strawberry jam and canning some berries for this winter. I had to stay clear of the house, the delicious aroma from the kitchen was enough to make me grab a jar of jam and a loaf of bread and hide out in the cider mill till both were gone. Hopefully, there would be strawberry shortcake tonight.

The bridge across Wolf Creek was about half complete. I watched as the men swarmed over the site, building a much-needed improvement to our community. The equipment was Army surplus machines rescued from Camp McCoy. All the material was supplied by the government and overseen by the Army Corps of Engineers. The noise and the dust could be seen and heard a mile away. The young men from the CCC Camp were happy to be working and earning money for their families. A year before, they had been living on handouts and eating at soup kitchens. Now they had hope for the future. The nation was pulling itself up by the bootstraps and going on about the business of living.

"I found it," Tom told us one morning. Tom had been relentless in tracking the bees to their hive.

Jake, Elmer, Hank and I were enlarging the fenced area for the chickens. We had the holes dug and were setting in the posts when Tom walked up from the woodlot.

"There's a big oak with the top broken off about twenty feet up. Looks like it's been that way for years. The tree has a big split about ten feet up that must have happened when the top came off. That's where the hive is."

Rubbing his chin, Jake said, "In 1920 there was a windstorm came through here. It tore the tops off a lot of trees. Might have happened then." All five of us set out for the woods. We watched the bees coming and going as we walked along. In the northwest corner of the woods stood the tall oak stump. The top looked like a giant hand had ripped the top off and split the tree halfway down. Singly and in pairs, the bees were coming and leaving the hive.

Lighting his pipe, Jake said, "The best time to pull that honeycomb out will be this fall. All the honey cells will be full, and the bees should be fairly quiet. Gonna need two ladders and my smoker." We watched a while longer then left the bees to their work.

The dark clouds rolled in pushed by gusty winds. Summer storms sometimes carried ominous warnings of things to come. This one brought the rain driven by winds at least forty-miles-per-hour.

A sudden banging on the roof startled Ardyce and me. It was hail bouncing off the new metal roof. Looking out the window, I could see hailstones as big as acorns covering the grass. As quickly as the storm had arrived, it passed over. The rain eased up, and soon it was gone. Within minutes, the sun was out, leaving the hail to evaporate in a light mist on the ground. No real damage was done to the orchard other than a few small branches broken off.

CHAPTER FIFTY-TWO

On a June night in 1933, Max Wilke closed his hardware store in Ladysmith and left by the back door. As he locked up, someone grabbed him by the shirt collar, and he stuck the back of his head with a hard object, sending him to his knees. Another pair of hands reached into his back pocket and lifted out his billfold. A bag that smelled of old potatoes was tied over his head.

Max heard someone running, then passed out. A short time later, Percy Braun was closing up his gasoline station when he was assaulted and robbed by two youths with handkerchiefs covering their faces from the nose down. He was knocked out and dragged around to the side of the station out of the light.

The same attempt was directed toward Cecil Roland closing up his grocery store, but Cecil was no push-over. A WWI veteran, Cecil had also been an amateur boxer in his youth. When the dust had settled, Alvin Hubert and Oscar Milton, both seventeen-years-old lay bleeding in the dirt. Cecil called the Sheriff, who arrested the boys. They later admitted to the two previous robberies, were tried and sentenced to three years at the Reformatory in Green Bay.

Standing on the Main street of Merrill with Reuben between us, Ardyce and I were watching the parade. It was the Fourth of July, and every business in town had a float entered. Elmer would be driving the REO truck with a banner on the back advertising WOLF CREEK CIDER. The hardware store, the feed mill, the lumber yard, all had colorful floats on wagons drawn by tractors or horses. The High School marching band was in fine form blasting out some of John Phillip Souza's famous songs. The local square dance group twirled around in bright attire, and even the bank had a small float.

The veterans of the Great War marched proudly in their uniforms waving small flags. Clowns in red and blue wigs, wearing big shoes, threw candy to the children. The fire department sounded the big horn on the pumper truck startling some of the horses. Melvin Hobart had mounted flags on his police car and waved to the crowd from the passenger seat while Luther drove.

The Mayor, Barton McCormick, riding in the back of black Cadillac convertible tossed out long stem roses from a box on the backseat. He was up for re-election this year.

When the parade wound down the crowd slowly broke up and made its way to the park by the Wisconsin River. Jake and Lilly already had two picnic tables butted together and were laying out food.

"Swings, Daddy, swings!" Reuben ran to the swing-set where June was watching over David and Louise. Elmer joined us followed by Melvin Hobart, Lucy Baxter, and Luther, who was carrying a large basket of food. Another picnic table was moved over and set up.

On the bandstand, a bluegrass string band was entertaining the crowd. Later, a popular polka band would play into the night. Jake and Melvin were entered in the horseshoe pitching contest. Elmer and Luther would again try to win the potato sack race. Last year they came in third.

No gathering is complete without a speech from a politician. The mayor welcomed everyone, then went into his re-election dialog. The city of Merrill was in great shape, he said. Businesses were thriving, and the economy was recovering. He praised the CCC Camps for the work they were doing. He promised to do his part to make the city great again. Most of the crowd knew the depression was not likely to be over soon. It would limp along until it slowly gained footing then begin to walk on its own.

As the day wound down, Ardyce and I gathered the children, said our goodbyes and drove home. Louise and David would spend the night with us so June and Elmer could have some fun dancing to the polkas.

The new bridge across Wolf Creek was finished! The gravel road had been widened and graded. Two autos could now pass without hugging the ditch. Pringle Construction, Archie, and his son, Elden, would arrive Monday to widen our drive and add a parking area.

Looking it over, Jake said, "Make it bigger. You need parking for the workers from town."

"I'll lose a lot of my nice green lawn if it's bigger," I told him.

"More parking space means more customers," he answered back. He was right of course, no sense arguing with

Jake when he was right. We also decided to use more of the white oak barrels this year. If we ran out or needed more, the distilleries were almost giving them away. The apples were almost ready for harvest. Another two weeks and we would be in full operation.

The campground had been improved over the summer. The Castor brothers had dug another well and installed a hand pump at the center of the campground. No more long trips to the house for water. The cider press was ready to go. A few small repairs had been made and new baskets added. A new spigot with a larger handle replaced the old one, and all the jugs and barrels were now labeled. Letters and telephone calls had confirmed orders from customers, including an order for apples for the CCC camp.

Hank and Tom would be joining them when the harvest was over. Mildred and Tom were a steady item now, and Hank was dating Mildred's sister, Lottie. Both men were renting a small house in Merrill, and the four took meals together. I sometimes caught Ardyce humming, 'here comes the bride' when she saw the four together. I hoped so.

CHAPTER FIFTY-THREE

"Let's make cider!" Luther hollered as the first bucket of apples went into the grinder. The tart smell of crushed apples drifted through the air. I loved it! I breathed it in deeply, savoring its aroma on the back of my tongue. At this moment, my thoughts were of my father, Reuben, and what he had given to Ardyce and me. Not just the house and the land, but a way of life we both loved. In the depths of a crippling depression, we were an island of contentment. We had good neighbors and many new friends, and all the credit went to my dad.

Jake, Elmer and I had pruned the orchard last fall and the apples this year seemed bigger and juicer than ever before. The cider flowed from the spigot into the jugs like nectar. Each day more families stopped to buy two or three jugs. The resorts added a few more gallons to their orders, and the Bristol Hotel in Merrill was now a regular customer. Our cider was fast becoming a well-known name across the entire state. I was seriously thinking about upgrading some of our equipment. The cider press itself was manufactured in 1889 in Manchester, England. If anything broke down, getting new parts could be a problem. An electric grinder was now available but was it reliable? I would be doing a lot of reading this winter.

Early morning in late September, the temperature was in the low forties. The perfect time to gather honey. Jake carried the smoker, I had a gallon bucket in each hand, Hank and Tom had the ladder, and Elmer toted a bag over his shoulder holding leather gloves, a hat with a net to cover the face, a jar of oil and rope.

The grass was wet with dew, and the sun was only a pink promise in the east. As we neared the tree, the soft, steady hum of the bees in the hive was like an invitation to us. Moving surely but quietly, Hank and Tom set the ladder against the oak tree. Jake took a folded sheet of newspaper from his pocket and placed it in the bottom of the smoker. A slow drip of oil was added until the paper was saturated. A handful of twigs went in next, then Jake fired up a match and dropped it in. The oil-soaked paper caught the flame and began to burn. Elmer gathered some green pine needles and slowly dropped them into the smoker. A light gray plume of smoke drifted out of the spout as more needles were added.

Setting the hat with the net on his head, Jake drew the drawstring at the bottom against his neck, buttoned his shirt at the top button and slid his hands into the gloves. The rope from the bag was uncoiled, revealing a small hook at one end. Draping the rope over his shoulder, Jake carefully climbed the ladder. When he reached the third to top rung he stopped, set the hook on the top rung and lowered the rest of the rope down. The hook was lowered and one of the buckets was attached and hauled up to the top.

With practiced slowness, Jake moved the smoker around inside the tree. With his other hand, he reached in and pulled out a dripping section of honeycomb which he laid in the bottom of the bucket. Several bees drifted in and out of the hole as pieces of their carefully crafted home was lifted out. When the bucket was about two-thirds full Jake motioned with his gloved hand to lower the bucket. When it settled to the ground, it was removed and the second bucket was lifted. Between the smoke and the cold morning air, the bees barely bothered Jake as he worked.

When the second bucket was half full, Jake motioned it down and slowly descended the ladder. The honey-soaked glove was removed, wrapped in a cloth and dropped into the bag along with the hat.

"One of the biggest honeycombs I have ever seen," Jake said with a smile.

"Did you leave some for them to build on?" Elmer asked.

Lighting his pipe, Jake answered, "I left about half the comb for them bees to build on. Next year we will have another big comb to harvest." Gathering everything up, we made our way back to the house.

The cider run was over, and the firewood for the coming winter was cut and stacked. It was time to say goodbye to Hank and Tom. They were going to join the Civilian Conservation Corps. There was a short period of training, and then they would be sent to one of the over two hundred camps in Wisconsin. Our new President's idea to put young men back to work was part of his National Recovery Act and seemed to be working well. A lot of roads, bridges, parks, and recreational areas were being built, and money was trickling into the economy again.

The newspaper finally delivered some good news. The president signed a bill repealing prohibition! The entire country had been waiting to hear this. Breweries and liquor distilleries had been getting ready to start production. This meant more men back to work and maybe an end to the gang wars in Chicago and New York.

Meanwhile, here on Wolf Creek Road, Elmer was out plowing the first snowfall. Ardyce was sewing more aprons, Reuben and Sam were napping on the bearskin rug, and I was thanking God for another wonderful year.

The End

ABOUT THE AUTHOR

Mark Gengler was born and raised on a small farm north of Medford, Wisconsin. He joined the U.S. Army in 1963 and was stationed at Fort Bragg, N.C., with the 82nd Airborne Division. He saw action in the Dominican Republic in 1965. After his discharge, he traveled America, working odd jobs in California, Texas, Colorado, Kansas City and New Orleans. He returned to Wisconsin and went to broadcasting school on the G.I. Bill. Mr. Gengler was a disc-jockey, got married, and went to work at the University of Wisconsin, Oshkosh, until retiring in 2003.

TITLES
by MARK GENGLER

NOAH THORNE
A WISCONSIN FARM BOY IN THE 1920'S

THANKS A LOT GOD

WOLF CREEK CIDER
THE STORY OF AARON STROUD